Thanksgiving Day PARADE

D. Allen

DN Publishing

Thanksgiving Day Parade
Copyright © 2024 by D. Allen
Batavia, NY

www.DavidNethBooks.com

ISBN: 978-1-963602-11-1
First Edition

Subscribe to the author's newsletter for updates and exclusive content:
DavidNethBooks.com/Newsletter

Follow the author at:
www.facebook.com/DavidNethBooks
www.instagram.com/dnpublishing

Also by D. Allen

Montana Beach

Summer Stay

Summer Job

Summer Nights

Small Town Christmas

A Christmas Reunion

A Christmas Charade

A Christmas Spark

A Christmas Song

A Christmas Departure

A Christmas Wedding

A Christmas Escape

A Christmas Renovation

A Christmas Family

Standalones

Snow After Christmas

Thanksgiving Day Parade

Chapter One
Thanksgiving Eve
Julie

Some people spend the night before Thanksgiving putting together everything they'd need to prepare the big feast the following day. Others sit back and enjoy a night off. Perhaps some frantically clean their houses for the arrival of extended family, or maybe run to the grocery store to see if they can find any more canned cranberry sauce.

Me? I avoided all of that. As much as I could.

"I'll take my usual," I told the bartender at my favorite local hangout on South Pearl Street.

Jim popped the top off a bottle of beer and set it on the bar. "Want me to start a tab, Jules?"

I passed him my debit card and nodded. "Of course!"

My plan was to stay out as long as I could to avoid the inevitable bickering between my mother and stepfather. It happened every night.

If it wasn't for the fact that she needed his salary to pay the mortgage and he needed her health insurance, I could pretty much guarantee the marriage would've crumbled a long time ago. Instead, they were trapped in this prison sentence, brought on by bureaucracy.

I've never been one for family time. We've never really been *tradition* people. Turkey and stuffing and going around the table to say how much we're thankful for wasn't really our thing.

The traditions I *did* enjoy, though? Spending time with people who are happy to see me. And after I snapped a quick picture of my beer bottle with the bar lights in the background, I grabbed it and stepped around the corner into the bowling alley, where three of my friends were just starting a game.

"Hey, cut me in!" I waved to my friends as I kicked off my shoes behind the bench and came around to greet them.

Brittany and Chloe both gave me hugs when they saw me. Eric was lined up like Fred Flintstone, all twinkle-toed and ready to hurl the ball down the lane. He did, and with a crash of pins, he tossed his hands up and roared, drawing all attention to him.

The lift of his shirt was hard to miss. He wasn't some muscle-chiseled model. His gut certainly showed that he liked beer. But his rugged handsomeness and overall charm made up for not having the perfect body. And that made my mind wonder about what the rest of his body looked like even more.

When he saw me, he cried out, "Julie!" and then wrapped his arm around me.

I put my arm around his bulk and leaned into him. His red beard tickled my face and some of my long blonde hair got tangled in it. I absently stroked my hair back into place when we parted, much sooner than I would've liked.

"You're late!" he said. "I've already got a strike on you!"

"We can add her in," Chloe said. "Each of us has only bowled once. Julie, if you want to play, it's your turn."

I nodded, then grabbed one of the balls in the return corral and stepped up to take my turn.

The marbled blue ball sailed down the lane and knocked out six pins. Not my best, but not my worst. I certainly needed warming up. My friends and I had tossed around the idea of joining a bowling league, but with me and Chloe being off to college and Brittany picking up as much overtime as she could manage, that really only left Eric and a few of our other drinking buddies, Tony and Otto. So, in a sense, the bowling league would have been a drinking league, making Eric and the other guys even more regulars of the bar than they already were.

"You're supposed to knock the pins down, Jules!" Eric cupped his hands around his mouth and shouted, as if he wasn't standing less than ten feet away from me. The hoarseness in his voice told me that he'd been shouting for a while. Clearly, he was already teetering on drunk. Factoring in his size and how often he drank, he must've started drinking at noon.

I tossed the ball down the lane a second time and knocked down two more pins. A total of eight. That was going to leave a mark on my score, compared to Eric's first-frame strike.

Chloe clapped her hands. "Good try, Jules!"

I retrieved my beer from the table, then found the picture I had taken of it on the bar and posted it to my Story. Then I snapped a picture of Brittany, who had stepped up to take her turn to bowl and posted that as well. Then, I leaned into Chloe and we both made kissing faces at the screen.

"Cute!" Chloe declared.

Another few presses on my screen, and that

picture was posted as well.

"Enough with the pictures, girls!" Eric said, with a fresh bottle of beer in his hand. "Jesus, this isn't a photoshoot."

I held up my phone and snapped one of him. He swiped at my phone and missed, resulting in a blurry picture of him. It looked artsy. I liked it.

"Sure, it is," I said. "Every day is a photo shoot!"

He tried again to take the phone from me, but I pulled it away in time, so he grabbed my wrist and spun me around so my back was pressed up against him. I giggled as we struggled, eventually sinking to the floor.

My heart fluttered with how close we were. There had been a lot more physical touches from Eric over the last couple months. I couldn't figure out whether he was flirting or not. Of course I wanted to *believe* that he was flirting, but my brain was telling me to put that wall up and not expect too much for fear of getting hurt.

"Looks like you're getting empty," Eric said.

My bottle was only halfway gone, but I recognized that it was an excuse to extract himself from the situation and avoid any further awkwardness.

Eric didn't do awkward.

In his absence, the game settled a bit. I took a seat next to Brittany while Chloe bowled.

"Are you dreading tomorrow as much as I am?" Brittany asked.

She had a perfectly normal family. A mom and a dad, two brothers, and even a family dog. But Brittany hated tradition and anything that made her feel normal. She felt trapped when she felt normal. Besides that, it was a forced day off from work for her, and when she was paid hourly, it mattered. She had wanted to go into work and get the holiday pay, but her mother had thrown a fit, so Brittany had no choice but to attend her traditional family Thanksgiving dinner, now laced with resentment between mother and daughter.

It wasn't quite the same situation as me, but it was still nice to commiserate with someone.

"Mm-hmm," I murmured. "Between my stepdad shouting at the stupid football game, my mother swearing and banging things around in the kitchen, and my brother being completely complacent to our messed up family, I would much rather skip the holiday."

"Right?" Brittany responded. "At least with Christmas we get gifts."

"*Then* there's a distraction," I said in agreement.

Chloe came back from the lane. "Where's Eric? He's up."

I nodded toward the bar. "Getting some refills. He'll be back."

"Again?" Chloe asked. "He just got another drink!"

Brittany nodded. "Just be glad Tony and Otto aren't here."

"Where are they again?" Chloe asked as she took a seat on the bench across from us.

"They're both traveling for Thanksgiving," Brittany said. "Tony's parents moved out to Tennessee — couldn't stand the New York taxes, I guess. Or maybe it was the weather. I don't know."

"And where's Otto?" I asked.

"They go up to his uncle's cabin in the Adirondacks every year for Thanksgiving to go hunting," she said. "The hunting season is a little different up there."

I nodded, then turned to my phone. "Well, it looks like Tony found a bar anyway." I leaned over and showed the girls a picture of Tony chugging from a beer can in some dark bar.

Chloe scoffed. "Typical." She was still nursing her first drink.

Brittany shrugged. "I mean, it *is* the night before Thanksgiving. That's, like, a drinking holiday. So I guess I get it today."

Chloe and I exchanged looks. We both disagreed

with Brittany about the drinking "holiday," but kept it to ourselves.

On one of the TVs hanging over the bowling lanes they were playing the nightly news. Was it the eleven o'clock? I had lost track of time. The footage showed a local marching band, while the words: LOCAL BAND TO MARCH IN THE THANKSGIVING DAY PARADE IN NYC scrolled across the bottom.

"Oh cool! One of the high school bands is going to be in the parade tomorrow." Chloe pointed to the screen. "Ugh, I can't wait to pour myself a cup of coffee and sit on the couch in my bathrobe and watch the parade with my sisters while the food cooks."

I nodded. "I do like the parade."

"I'm usually still passed out then," Brittany muttered. "If I'm going to have to take a day off, I better do it in a haze."

"I've always wanted to see it in person," I said, ignoring Brittany's comments.

"See what in person?" Eric asked as he came back with a pitcher of beer and plastic cups.

"The Thanksgiving Day Parade," I told him. "It would make the *perfect* Thanksgiving. Especially considering my Thanksgivings usually suck."

Brittany nodded. "That would be cool. I'd love to pass out the candy to the kids."

"I'd want to be on a float and wave to the kids," Chloe said.

Eric laughed. "Yeah, and I'd like to cut the ties to the balloons and let them all go."

The girls laughed, but I interjected a fun fact I had just learned about from a video I saw in my feed. "Actually, back in the day before they cared about pollution, that's exactly what they used to do with the big balloons."

"Now *that* would be something to see." Brittany pulled a plastic cup and filled it from the pitcher.

"Those streets are probably *mobbed*," Chloe said. "Could you imagine how long people are waiting just to get a glimpse of the parade?"

"Especially when you can just watch it at home in your underwear." Eric sloppily poured himself another drink.

"I don't know," I said, trying to get the image of Eric in his underwear out of my head. "The parade route is a couple miles long. I think the crowd might not be that bad. It's not like it's New Year's Eve or anything."

"Still, those floats probably have to be registered *way* in advance," Chloe said. "I wonder if there's a waiting list to get in the parade. Or a fee—I'm sure there's a fee. There's always a fee with everything nowadays."

"Free marketing," I added. "But I'm not sure it'd be terribly hard to get on one. I see random people on those floats next to celebrities and characters all the time."

Chloe shook her head. "They're not random, Jules. They're probably a part of the team for that float—someone who works for the company but doesn't have camera time. Someone who isn't a household name. I think half the time the celebrities are the ones who are random just so they can help advertise the parade."

"Which then advertises the company." Brittany rolled her eyes. "It's all a big marketing scam, and we're falling into it."

I turned back to the TV, which had moved on to a statement about new street parking rules for the upcoming winter season.

I didn't want to believe that the parade was just a marketing gimmick. I mean, yes, of course, that was the main purpose when the parade had first started, but since then it had evolved into so much more than that. A sense of community for the whole country, which spawned millions of tiny moments of families creating traditions and memories around it over the last several decades.

"Either way," Chloe said, breaking into my thoughts. "Those people on the floats aren't just nobodies. They're real people, working hard for their companies, who deserve to be in the limelight, even if for only a few seconds a year."

"They might as well be nobodies," Eric said. "I don't know them and I don't give a shit about any of them. I don't even watch the parade. No point."

"Would you watch it if you knew someone in the parade?" I asked him.

He scoffed. "Yeah, like *that's* ever going to happen!"

The idea of Eric watching the parade at home in his underwear, as he so eloquently stated, was still stuck in my head.

"I'm just saying, I don't think it'd be that hard to get on a float," I said. "I could do it."

Brittany narrowed her eyes. She was growing skeptical of my bravado. "Okay, well, if it's not that hard then why haven't you done it?"

I averted my eyes. Where was I going with that statement anyway? It wasn't like I was ever going to get to be in the parade. Especially not when there was less than twelve hours before it started.

"Oh, I bet you could do it." Eric wrapped his arm around me and tugged me closer.

The physical touch made my heart race, but also left disappointment seeping through my veins. He gave me the awkward side-hug that he gave to

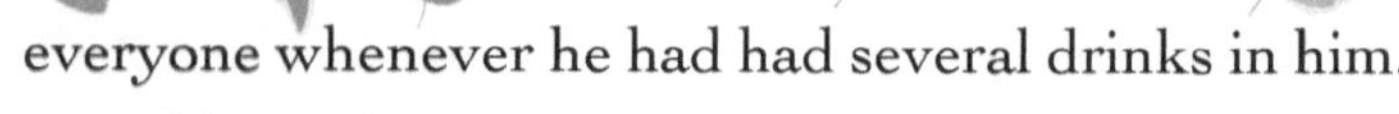

everyone whenever he had had several drinks in him.

Chloe rolled her eyes. "None of you are listening to me. All of this is decided on *well* in advance! They're not just seat-fillers walking down the street in one of the biggest parades in the country!"

"In fact," Eric went on, clearly ignoring Chloe. "I *dare* you to get on a float."

Brittany broke out into a wide grin and *oohed*. "Oh man! Now you *have* to do it!" It was possible that Brittany had had too much to drink as well. "Wait, wait, wait!" She pulled out her phone and began recording me. "Julie Griffiths, do you accept the dare to get on a float in the Thanksgiving Day Parade by the end of the parade tomorrow morning?"

I froze. I couldn't turn the dare down. Not with their scrutinizing eyes on me. Not with it being recorded—which I knew would be posted immediately with my handle being tagged. Everyone online would see it as well.

"Jules, you don't have to," Chloe said from beside Brittany.

"Of course she does!" Eric blurted. "She's been *dared*."

Another moment passed, then I recovered and put on some confidence—even though it was fake. "What's my reward if I do it?"

There were several more *oohs* from around. The group of guys bowling next to us had taken interest in our conversation. Not sure how, being that Brittany and Eric were making me a spectacle and all.

Eric considered my question, then said, "I'll pay for your drinks for the rest of your life—*if* you can pull it off."

Another round of *oohs* erupted from the peanut gallery.

If Eric was my drink bitch for the rest of my life, then I would have a reason to call him up out of the blue to come and buy me a drink. I would have a reason to text him, to tease him, to spend more time with him. But I needed to make it more personal. "I need at least one meal a week in there, too."

"Greedy, huh?" Eric asked with a smirk.

I smiled back, playful. Pushing the limits of our game of cat and mouse. "Hey, a girl's gotta eat."

"Fine." Eric stuck out his hand. "*If* you can do it, you'll have one meal a week on me and drinks for life."

I smiled and shook his hand. "Then you have a deal."

Chapter Two
Thanksgiving Eve
Brian

"**B**abe, stop!" Kendra sobbed as she tugged on Brian's arm.

He ignored her and continued to shove as many of his clothes into a single duffel bag as he could fit. There were so many other things that were his throughout the apartment, but those would have to wait. Right now he just needed to get out.

"Won't you please *talk* to me?" she pleaded.

With effort, he zipped up his bag. It was nearly bursting at the seams. When he finally got it zipped closed, he slung it over his shoulder and brushed past her through the bedroom door.

"I'm sorry!" she wailed. "Brian, I'm sorry! I'm sorry I

messed everything up. If I could go back and change it all, I would!"

He stopped in the bathroom and grabbed his toothbrush and retainers—nothing about this was the clean getaway that he had been hoping for. But then, reality was usually different than TV. The truth of the matter was, without the retainers he had gotten at sixteen, the gap between his two front teeth would rear its ugly head within two days.

Salt in the wound.

His computer lay on the table beside the couch. He scooped it up and tried to find a place in his bag to shove it in. Everything was jam packed. And then there was his charger. He unplugged it from the wall, but felt resistance on the other end.

Kendra.

She looked at him with red, puffy, wet eyes, and held onto the other end of his charger. "I won't let you go until you talk to me."

He pulled on the cord, but she refused to let it go.

"Please, Brian," she said. "Stay here so we can talk this out."

Another shot against her. She had clearly forgotten that he had planned to go back home for Thanksgiving anyway. The bus ticket had been booked weeks ago. The implosion of their relationship had only removed the necessity of missing each other.

Her dark hair hung limply around her face, which was swollen and wet with tears. She really was an ugly crier. "I love you. I never wanted to hurt you."

The rage he had been shoving down erupted inside him, spilling out of his mouth.

"That's a lie!" He pointed right at her face. "You knew exactly what you were doing. So don't sit there and pretend like you didn't expect all of this to happen."

"I know! You're right! It was a mistake! I know that. But that doesn't mean we need to give up on this. On us."

"What part of my reaction came as a surprise, Kendra? Huh?" He raised his eyebrows, waiting for an answer, but none came.

"I'm sorry," she said.

"You're sorry you got caught. You *might* even be sorry that you hurt me. But you're not sorry for what you did, because you knew what you were doing all along. You made the choice, Kendra. Now you have to live with it. So all of this guilt and shame you feel, you deserve it." With another tug on the cord, it slipped from her hands.

"Okay—okay! I'm a terrible person! I did this to myself. You're right. You're right about all of it. But can't you give me a second chance? Can't we make this work?"

He wasn't sure there was any recovering from this scar in their relationship. Nor did he care to find out. He could hardly stand to look Kendra in the face for another second without seeing what she had done.

"Goodbye, Kendra," he said simply.

Without another word, he gathered his overstuffed bag, laptop, and cord, and stepped out of the apartment into the hallway, slamming the door behind him.

It wasn't until he made it down to the lobby that he found a bench nearby and opened his bag to move things around. He shoved his laptop and charging cord inside, then put his weight on it while he forced the zipper to close. It pulled at the seams, but held.

There was a train stop not far from their apartment—Kendra's apartment now. He didn't live there anymore.

He got on the train, rode it downtown to Union Station, then got in line to board a bus to New York City. A nine hour ride. One that would travel overnight, thankfully.

Toronto was the start of the bus line, so when he and the other passengers got on, they all had plenty of room in their seats. That would change with each city they stopped in along the way to the Big Apple.

Brian set his bag on the empty seat next to him,

then put up his hood and leaned against the window as it pulled away from the station.

The intent was to sleep, but his mind was spinning with having his whole world turned upside down that he knew sleep would be impossible.

He would have to move back home. Back in with his mother until he could find a place on his own. And, depending on how long it took him to extract his life from Kendra's, his mother would be his roommate for a while until he saved enough to rent his own apartment. And it wasn't like real estate in New York was cooling down anytime soon.

He would have to notify work, tell them he was coming back into the office after spending the last year working remotely. He would have to arrange another trip back to Toronto to get the rest of his stuff from the apartment. Clothes, books, several dishes, food he had helped pay for.

On second thought, he realized it was all replaceable. Anything of sentimental or significant monetary value was stuffed into the duffel bag beside him. His whole world crammed into one small little bag.

The bus slowed as the lanes in the road narrowed for the checkpoint to cross the border. Yet another step forward toward home. Toward his new life. Toward his family.

How was he going to break the news to his family? His mother adored Kendra. His brothers got along nicely with her. They had all talked about vacationing together, seeing each other for the holidays, and even doing other things together.

Thanksgiving dinner was going to be awkward.

Brian shifted in his seat as the bus lurched forward, then braked again, then lurched forward yet again. Inching forward little-by-little until the driver was finally given the approval to enter the country.

That was another thing on his to-do list: talk to immigration about ending his Canadian visa early. Brian shook his head in disappointment—embarrassment. He would have to be reminded of the things he had done to make things work with Kendra. The lengths he had gone to for that woman. All in the name of love. What a crock that turned out to be.

Not only had he moved away from his family, but he had moved to a whole different *country*—they had even discussed him applying for dual citizenship when the two of them got married.

Yeah. That definitely wouldn't be happening.

In another thirty minutes, the bus pulled up to the first stop in the United States: Buffalo.

Brian sat back and pretended he was asleep,

hoping that nobody would be willing to wake him to claim the seat beside him. Besides, it was the first stop so there were still plenty of other seats that people could take. The tactic had worked on previous trips home.

The noise level on the bus increased as people found their seats, but fifteen minutes later everyone settled. And Brian still had an empty seat beside him. At least he'd be able to get *some* sleep until the next stop in Rochester.

It was late. The overnight trips were usually not as popular as the daytime ones. Most people were more willing to sacrifice a perfectly good day in order to travel than they were to sacrifice a good night's sleep.

Brian cracked his eyes open, chancing a glance at the front. The driver was back in his seat and pulling on his seatbelt.

Home free.

Brian closed his eyes and settled back into his seat. He tried to get comfortable again, but then he heard someone talking at the front. Probably passengers trying to get comfortable and discuss seating arrangements with the strangers they needed to sit by. Brian didn't focus on what they were saying.

The bus began to pull away.

Someone nudged his shoulder. "Excuse me. Can

you please move your bag? There aren't any other seats."

His eyes flicked open and he saw a girl standing there. Probably only a few years younger than him. She had a large purse on her shoulder and she stood holding the back of the seat to steady her.

She was beautiful. Blonde hair that hung around her face, and clear blue eyes that seemed to shine, even in the nighttime dark.

But the last thing he needed at the moment was to be admiring another woman. He just wanted to be alone—to disappear from the world for a couple hours. But so far, being alone had only left him trapped by his thoughts. Maybe a passenger would help him focus on other things than letting his mind run rampant on the journey home.

"Lady, let's go! Take a seat!" the driver called from the front.

The girl turned to him with those perfect blue eyes, pleading.

Brian grumbled and sat up, pulling his heavy bag onto his lap. As the girl settled in beside him, Brian felt even more cramped in the window seat.

Between the tight confines and his running thoughts, there was certainly going to be no sleeping tonight.

Chapter Three
Thanksgiving Eve
Julie

The seats were so uncomfortable. I tried several times to readjust, finding minimal comfort on my side. The problem was, when I lay like that, I was too close to the guy sitting next to me, who was *clearly* not happy about having to share his seat.

As if it was my fault.

Finally, I got too tired of trying to get comfortable and resigned myself to the idea that I wouldn't be sleeping, like I'd hoped. Whatever alcohol I'd had at the bar had worn off. Eric, Brittany, and—begrudgingly—Chloe all chipped in for my Uber to the airport, where the Buffalo bus stop was. I had just managed to arrive by midnight, when the bus was about to pull away. Luckily,

I had the ticket information on my phone and the driver let me on.

Throughout the bus, everyone was quiet, even though it seemed that nobody could properly get to sleep. Sure, most people had their eyes closed and were *trying*, but the way each of them moved every few seconds said that their efforts were futile.

Even the guy sitting next to me was tossing and turning, trying to find a way to get comfortable sitting upright in his seat with his bag sitting in his lap.

I felt guilty for taking the empty seat next to him but it was the last one.

Well, actually, no. It wasn't the last one. There were two up near the front. One next to a guy who looked a little *too* excited at the prospect of a young college girl sitting next to him, and one next to a woman who had enough B.O. to fill the front of the bus.

That left the semi-attractive guy in the back. The one who very much did not want to share his seat. Too bad.

My phone rang, and several people turned and gave me dirty looks. I silenced it, then looked around. There were no signs that said that talking *wasn't* allowed. And it wasn't like I was going to talk as loud as I could.

So I answered.

"Hey," Chloe said on the other end. "I wanted to talk to you about that dare. I know we chipped in to Uber you to the airport, and I know you bought a ticket, but…" She took a deep breath. "Don't do it, Jules. It was just a stupid joke that Eric made. One he's probably not even going to remember in the morning. Currently, he's passed out in a booth in the bar."

It was quiet on the other end, so I assumed that Chloe stepped outside to make the call. It was kind of strange to think that they were still at the bar and I was on my way to the biggest city in the country in the middle of the night.

"Well, even if I *did* want to turn around, Chloe, your timing is terrible," I said. "I'm already on the bus. We already left."

Chloe was quiet for minute, followed only by a single, "Oh."

"Yeah," I murmured. The lady across the aisle from me continued to glare at me. As if my phone call was bothering her ability to listen to her earbuds. I was talking quietly, and the roar of the bus motor was loud enough as it was.

"Look, I'll split the bus fare with you if you want to get on a bus right away to come back," Chloe offered. "Or if you get off at the next city, I can drive

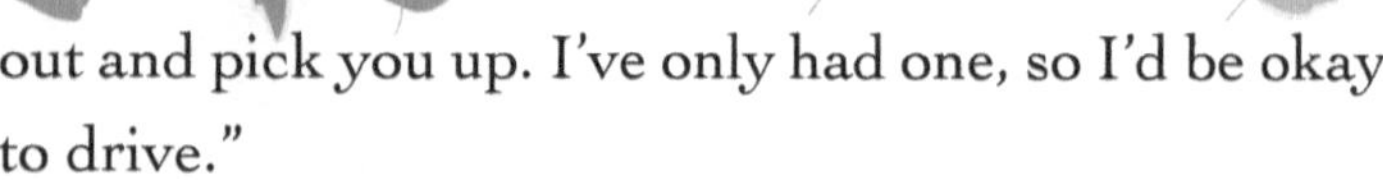

out and pick you up. I've only had one, so I'd be okay to drive."

"No, Chloe, I don't want you to risk it. Besides, this is something I want to do. I bet you the first thing Eric asks when he wakes up is where the remote is so he can watch it on TV." There was more silence on the other end, so I added, "Come on, Chloe! You and I both know I dread any holiday with my family. It's not like I'm missing anything with this one. Let me make this Thanksgiving a memorable one."

Chloe sighed again. "I can't talk you out of this?"

"I don't think so."

"And you're going to be safe?"

"I promise."

"And you'll call me if you get into trouble?"

"Anytime."

"And you'll have fun?"

I cracked a smile. "That's the plan."

"Then I guess I can't stop you. Be careful, Jules."

"I will. Thanks, Chloe."

I tucked my phone back in my bag and then tried to relax. Chloe had given me an out and I stuck firm with my decision.

But was it the right one? I had never even been to New York City. Maybe Chloe was right. Maybe I should just get off in Rochester and call for a ride home.

Of course, if I called my mother, I would have to be subjected to the wrath of her and my stepdad, making Thanksgiving dinner even more unbearable than I had already expected it to be. Not to mention the endless scrutiny from my brother. And I would never be able to show my face in the bar again. Any chance at anything more with Eric would certainly be out the window. I should've suggested that he and I both come to get on the float instead of jetting off by myself and leaving him alone with Brittany.

How stupid was I?

Nope. I wasn't going to go there. I needed to change my thoughts. I *would* be successful at this. And if I wasn't? I'd have one hell of a story to tell.

The guy beside me shifted in his seat again. He clearly was not catching any Zs. When he turned and saw me looking at him, he scrunched his eyebrows together as if to say, "What are you looking at?"

Instead, I smiled and offered my hand. "Hi, I'm Julie."

He glared at me, but sat up straighter, adjusting the bag in his lap, then pulled his hood off and shook my hand. "I'm Brian." He turned back to the window, not engaging in anymore conversation.

"Where are you headed to?" I asked.

"New York," he murmured, eyes still trained out the window. We couldn't see much in the darkness.

Only a few passing cars with their headlights trained right in front of them.

"Oh wow! That's where I'm going too! Are you going for the parade?"

Another glare in my direction, then, "No, I'm going home for Thanksgiving."

My eyes widened. "You *live* in New York City?" My voice was louder than I expected and several people around us cleared their throats, which had nothing to do with the chillier temperatures springing up illnesses.

Of course I knew that New York City had a population of over eight million people, but I hadn't really met anyone my own age from there. Sure, I had met people from *down state* in college, but they seemed to be from the outskirts of "the city."

Or maybe it was that they told me the names of places within the city and I just didn't know where those places were. Until Eric had challenged me, I had had no real interest in going to New York City. So much had changed in such little time.

"Uh…yeah, I guess that's where I live now." He seemed to sober as he considered my question. With his hood off, I could see that he was more than just *semi*-attractive. Still, his attitude was off-putting.

"You guess?" I asked. "Are you, like, moving or something?"

Another pause as he considered. "Yeah, I guess I am." He turned his body back toward the window, quietly telling me that he didn't want to talk.

That never bothered me. I laughed a little to myself. "You guess a lot."

He shrugged.

I fiddled with the strap on my bag. "Well, I'm going to New York City on a dare to see if I can get on a float in the parade."

Brian looked over at me. "You mean the big televised one?"

"Mm-hmm," I said with a nod.

"You're crazy."

Now it was my turn to shrug. As he continued to look at me with wild eyes, I laughed again. "I know I'm crazy. And that this idea is a little wild —"

"A *little* wild?"

"What's the worst that can happen?"

"The worst that can happen is that you get arrested."

My lips formed into a giant *O* as the realization hit me. *Of course* there would security and police patrolling throughout the parade. Any violators, no matter how innocent, would have to face legal repercussions. Was I making a mistake? I supposed it was too late to back down now.

Brian sighed and sat up. "Here's what you need to do: find a float that has costumed characters — but only the ones who stand and wave. You don't want the ones who have to dance or anything. Then, if you can convince one of them to let you wear their costume instead of them, you can sneak on the float undetected."

"You think it's that easy?"

"I wouldn't say it's *easy*, but I think that's your best bet. Those people in the costumes probably go to the parade every year. All they want is the paycheck. As long as you're not taking that from them, then sure, I think you could swing it."

I smirked, glad that I hooked him into a conversation so I didn't have to sit alone. "The trouble is, in order for me to win the dare, my friends need to be able to see me on camera. If I put on a character costume, they won't be able to see me unless I take the costume off — and scar millions of children watching in the process."

Brian laughed at that. "Who even proposed this dare?"

Now it was my turn to look away. "Just a friend of mine."

"Well, it sounds like they were setting you up to fail by creating all of these rules."

"He didn't set *rules*," I blurted. "But it makes

sense that he needs to be able to see me in order to know I was there."

"He can't just take your word for it?"

My shoulders began to raise up. "Well...I don't know..."

"Sounds to me like you could've snapped a few pictures and sent them as proof enough. Your friend doesn't trust that you won't cheat?"

"Okay, *stranger*, you don't need to be critiquing my life—and my *friends*, who you don't even know!"

"Fine, I won't critique your friends, but I'll critique their stupid idea. It's stupid."

I raised my eyebrows. "Wow. What a great comeback."

"I'm not really sure how to dumb it down anymore."

I rolled my eyes. Now I was regretting striking up a conversation with this arrogant jerk. "Never mind." I turned away from him and focused on the man who was sleeping three rows up. It looked like he was about to fall out of his seat and into the aisle. I wondered how many bumps in the road or sudden turns it would take to get him to topple over.

"Look," Brian said from beside me. "I'm sorry for saying this idea is stupid—don't get me wrong, I still think that. I'm just sorry for saying it out loud."

"Is this supposed to be an apology?"

"Of sorts. If you're really dead-set on doing this, I guess I can help you figure out how."

"Really?" I was suddenly more excited than I expected. The burden of having to figure it all out on my own had been weighing on me and I didn't even realize it until someone offered relief. I didn't know the city. I didn't know how the parade was planned. I didn't know how I was going to pull this off. I didn't really know anything.

He nodded. "Yep. You need a new plan."

"That's it? That's your big advice?"

"Can you blame me? I've never even thought of doing something so stupid before. And you've given me — what? — five minutes to figure this out for you?"

I rolled my eyes again and turned back to the man about to topple over. His neck was jarred in such an uncomfortable position that I wondered briefly if he might be dead. But then he snorted and shifted a little, proving that life was still present. A Thanksgiving miracle.

"Let me think about this," Brian muttered from beside me. "Maybe you can hang around the parade starting point to look for an opening."

I looked over at him. "The parade starting point?"

"Well, yeah. It has to start somewhere, right?"

"I guess I never really thought about it. But sure,

that sounds about right."

He narrowed his eyes. "You haven't put any thought into this at all, have you?"

"I've known about this for—" I checked the time on my phone. "—only about three hours!"

"You were only dared three hours ago and now you're on a bus across the state? That's a little…impulsive."

I shrugged. "Sometimes you have to be impulsive. That's where the best stories come from, right?"

He didn't say anything, but the expression on his face said enough. He was judging me. Hardcore.

Then again, even I could agree that this plan, in hindsight, *was* kind of stupid. But my pride wouldn't let me admit that out loud.

"Yes, there's a parade starting point," Brian went on. "If you head up there, they're probably using some of the park to—"

"Central Park," I cut in, boasting my little knowledge of New York City.

"Yes…" he said slowly, then added, "Do you have any idea where the parade route starts?"

"Central Park," I said with a proud smile.

"You do realize that Central Park stretches, like, fifty blocks, right? It's huge."

"And?"

"And you can't just say it starts at the park, you

need to know *where* in the park."

"Do *you* know where?" I pressed. Mr. Smarty-Pants was flaunting his knowledge now. I wasn't a dumb girl. Okay, sure, maybe this trip wasn't my most shining example of a *good* idea, but I was certainly smarter than it seemed.

"Central Park West and 78th Street," he said. "Near the museum."

"And you just *happened* to know that?"

He looked a little defensive. "I was reading an article about it the other day and I thought it was interesting."

A man who read. Who had ever heard of that?

"Do you have any idea where that is?" he asked.

"The park!" I said with a laugh.

He closed his eyes, took a deep breath, and gently nodded. "Yes. By the park. Have you even been to New York before?"

"I live in New York," I said.

"I meant New York *City*."

"Oh! No."

He shook his head. "You're going to need more help than just coming up with a plan."

I smiled. "You seem like you know your way around town, being that you're a New Yorker and all. Why don't you help me?" As I said the words, I wondered if I would regret them. Then again, it wasn't as if I hadn't been around arrogance before. My defense mechanism to that was to deflect to humor.

"I don't…" he started, but then stopped when my face began to droop with disappointment. It hadn't been my intent to guilt him into it, but I couldn't help the look on my face as all my wildest dreams came crashing down with his denial.

We were quiet as the proposal, and the beginning of a rejection, hung in the air between us.

Finally, he said, "Okay. I'll help you. But you need to trust my advice."

"Done."

"And you need to listen."

"We'll see."

"And if the police start poking around, I'm out."

"Understandable." I smiled again and offered my hand for the second time. "So…do we have a deal?"

He let out a heavy breath of air, then took my hand. "Fine. Deal."

It was the second deal I made that night. But I felt good about this one.

Chapter Four
Thanksgiving
Brian

The passengers were all bleary-eyed and tired from the long, uncomfortable journey across New York State. Brian stepped off and heard the hiss of brakes from buses, the sounds of the subway rolling beneath them, and—most of all—smelled the stench of the streets.

Home. Flaws and all.

Since neither of them had stowed bags under the bus, Brian led Julie away from the gathering crowd alongside the bus and talked over his shoulder.

"Everyone is probably starting to gather for the parade now..." He trailed off when he realized that Julie was no longer behind him. He searched the crowd until he found her.

Down the street a little ways, she had her phone raised up and was taking pictures of the skyscrapers that made up Hudson Yards. Then she turned her camera toward her and began to talk to it. Over the noise of the city, he couldn't make out what she was saying, but by the way she was acting he knew that she looked like easy prey for pickpockets—or worse—if he left her alone.

Marching over to her, he came up just as Julie was signing off on her video.

"What are you doing?" he asked.

"Look!" she cheered. Her hand extended to something behind Brian. "It's the High Line! I've seen all kinds of cool posts about this. Let's go!"

Brian shook his head. "No. We don't have time."

Julie's attention was on her phone. She tapped at the screen, posting the pictures to her feed and the video to her Story.

"If we're going to pull this off, we can't start sightseeing," he said.

Pictures posted, she slid her phone in her pocket and gave him a skeptical look. "I *think* we have enough time to walk down the High Line and get up to the park. I mean, it's not that far. We can just get a cab."

"And pay how much for that?"

She shrugged. "I don't know."

He shifted the strap of the bag on his shoulder, then crossed his arms. "You really have no idea where anything is in the city, do you?" That fact continued to astound him. Sure, he knew of plenty of people who visited the city with the same level of naïvety, but they usually had a plan. Julie was completely winging it.

Another shrug from her. "I've never really been interested in New York City before, but now that I'm here, it's amazing." Her eyes lifted to the skyscrapers again.

"Word of advice: if you want to avoid being pickpocketed, walk with a purpose. That means don't stare at the tall buildings!"

Julie rolled her eyes.

Brian put up his hands. "Okay. Fine. Don't believe me. I'm only looking out for you. I've only grown up my whole life in the city—but hey, you're right. Some country girl who lives her life on her phone knows more than I do."

"I never said that," she shot back. "And low blow about my phone, dude. Don't profile me like that."

"What part did I get wrong?"

She looked away from him. "I don't live my life in my phone. I use it to *document* my life."

"And the difference?"

"Look, just because I stop to enjoy the things around me by taking pictures and videos of them—which I share with my followers—does not make me a shallow person. Now, if you're going to continue to judge me like this, then I guess we're done here."

Brian held his tongue. He was annoyed that she was right. He was harshly judging her, and that wasn't fair. And he *had* offered to help her, which he didn't have to do. He didn't need to make it a miserable experience for both of them.

He could've just as easily given up on her—let her wander the city for all he cared. But there were two things keeping him glued to Julie's side.

For one, he could tell that Julie wouldn't last one day in the city by herself. She was like a curious puppy, chasing after one thing, then another until she had completely lost all sense of where she was. And that would only set her up to be an easy target for those who might want to hurt her. As annoying as she could be, he certainly didn't want her to end up as another statistic.

The other reason was that Julie gave him the perfect excuse to avoid the awkward conversation with his family of what had happened between him and Kendra. Normally he would be happy to see his family—and he still was—but Julie's crazy dream also offered an opportunity for him to escape his life for a little while. Even if she was a little insufferable.

"Are you ready?" he asked after their standoff. He wasn't going to apologize for voicing his opinion. Instead, he just wanted to move on from it.

"Okay, *fine*," she said with a groan. "But can we go sightseeing after we get in the parade? I've never been to the city before and I'd hate to pass all of this up. I'm sure the leaves in the park look *beautiful*! My followers would love it!"

He led her to the corner. They had to cross the street to get to the subway stop at Hudson Yards. From there, they'd have to take the subway to the Port Authority stop, then wait for the E train to the 50th Street stop. They'd still have a walk to his mother's apartment, but it'd be better than walking it the entire way.

"You can do whatever you want," he said. "After we get on the float—assuming we aren't arrested— I'm going home to have turkey and pie with my family."

"You're just going to ditch me?" She raced to keep up with him amidst the distractions of the city.

"I won't be ditching you. We'll be parting on good terms, having accomplished what we set out to do. Strangers parting in the night."

"Isn't it supposed to be two *ships passing* in the night?"

Brian stopped and thought about it. She was right. "You get the point."

They crossed the street and Brian led her to the subway stop and began to descend the stairs. The noise of the traveling trains picked up and he felt the rush of air over his face from the movement through their tunnels. And, of course, the lower they got, the worse the smell became.

"So where are we going now?" Julie asked loudly over the noise. "Oh, and what is that *smell*?"

"That's the city," Brian said, then added, "We're going back to my house."

He led her to the emergency exit entrance, swiped his card, then held the door open for her. It was an old trick, to use the same card for two people. Especially a newcomer like Julie.

"Your house?" Her face showed surprise as she walked through the door. He pushed it closed behind them.

"Yeah." He marched on to the train platform. "Well, my *apartment*. Same thing."

"I thought you were going to help me?"

"I am."

"Oh, so we don't have time to sightsee, but we have time to stop home?"

Out of the corner of his eye, he saw her snapping pictures of the oncoming train. They arrived just in time.

The train's brakes squealed as it came to a stop, then there was a hissing sound as the door locks were released and the sliding door opened. Several travelers stepped out and carried on throughout the platform.

Since it was the last stop on the line, Brian and Julie stepped on to a mostly-empty train. Brian stood near the door. Their stop was only one stop away, but he knew the train would sit at the end for a while so the driver could switch to the other side of the train.

"I need to drop off my bag," Brian told her.

Julie scoffed. "It can't be that heavy."

Pulling his bag off his shoulder, he held it out to her.

"What? You want me to see for myself?" she asked.

"Go ahead," he encouraged her.

She reached for it and he let go, and the weight of the bag nearly knocked her to the floor of the train. He caught her with one hand, and reached for the bag with the other and ended up grabbing ahold of the hand she held the strap with in the process.

They hung there for a moment, both of them lost in each other's eyes. Julie's, Brian noticed again, were blue, which was really no surprise considering her blonde hair, but there was something about them

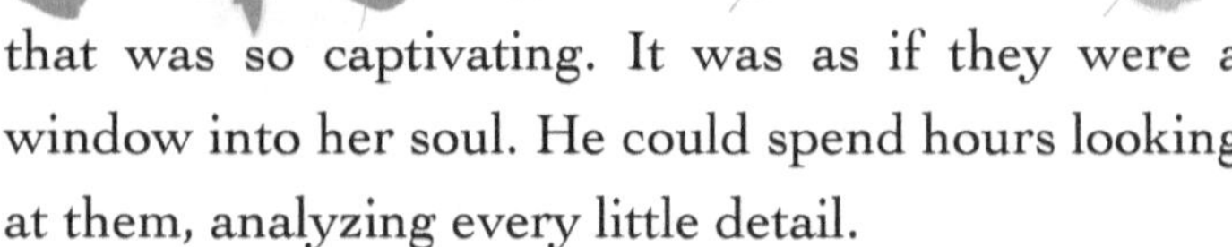

that was so captivating. It was as if they were a window into her soul. He could spend hours looking at them, analyzing every little detail.

As more passengers stepped on the train, Brian remembered where they were and promptly stood up and helped Julie right herself as well. Both of them averted their eyes from one another while they fussed with things that didn't need fussing.

Brian strapped his bag back over his shoulder while Julie straightened out her jean jacket and adjusted her purse on her own shoulder.

"Well." Julie cleared her throat. "I, uh, I guess you were right. We should take your bag back home. And it's perfect timing because I have to pee."

He couldn't help but smile. Such a direct way of expressing her need to take care of some bodily business was a sign of her personality coming back out to diffuse the awkwardness of the situation.

But then another thought struck Brian: Julie was going to have to come upstairs with him when he dropped off his bag. She was going to have to come into his mother's apartment and meet his family.

Hopefully his brothers hadn't arrived yet. His one brother, and his wife, lived in Queens, while his other brother, and his wife and kids, lived north of the city in Tarrytown. Neither was too terribly far, but they may have traveled early to avoid the hustle and bustle of the holiday crowd.

Even if his brothers *weren't* at the apartment yet, Julie would for sure meet his mother, who had likely already begun cooking Thanksgiving dinner—otherwise they wouldn't be eating until ten o'clock at night.

Brian's mother had loved Kendra—his whole family did, really. What would they say when they saw him come in with another girl? Some girl he didn't even know? They would make assumptions for sure.

For a moment, he debated whether he should just hold on to his bag while he went to the park with Julie, but it was killing his back. After traveling all night with it, he just wanted to get it off of him. A weight unloaded. A memory of his breakup with Kendra pushed aside.

He checked the time again. Just after seven. It was still early. If they moved quick, maybe they could avoid seeing his brothers and catch his mom while she was in the shower or maybe even still sleeping.

The odds were not in his favor.

"So, uh, have you ever been to the parade?" Julie asked, once again breaking the silence that fell between them. She probably believed it was from their clumsy encounter. Not that that wasn't playing a role in Brian's growing anxiety.

"Not in person, no."

"You've seen it elsewhere?"

He shook his head. "Only on TV."

"But you live right in New York…"

He cast her a look. "New Yorkers tend to avoid large gatherings that are really only seen on TV. The Thanksgiving Day Parade, New Year's Eve—Times Square in general." He shrugged. "Things like that don't really appeal to any of us locals."

"The tourist traps."

"Well…yeah."

She raised her eyebrows and studied him. "Sounds like you're a little conceited."

"Says the one who has been snapping selfies ever since we got off the bus."

At the moment, Julie had her phone pointed to the subway map on the wall of the train. At his words, she slipped her phone back into her back pocket. "Touché, Brian."

Above them, the robotic voice rang out, "Stand clear of the closing doors!"

The lights above the doors flashed and there were soft beeps, followed by a low hiss as the doors gently closed. With a jerk, the train launched into motion— which launched Julie right back into Brian again. He had braced himself with one of the bars in the center of the train car.

As she righted herself, she again diverted her eyes away from his. The day was going to be full of tension if they kept having more bumbling encounters like that.

Neither of them said anything the whole ride. The whooshing sound of the traveling train made it difficult to have a private conversation.

At the first stop, Brian caught Julie's attention, then nodded to the door and they walked out onto the platform together. They followed the signs for the E train, then waited a few minutes in silence until it came barreling down the tunnel.

Several people walked out, then Brian and Julie stepped in. The plus side of riding the train so early in the morning on a holiday was that there weren't as many people on as there normally were. Plus, they were taking the local train, which didn't usually have as many people as the express trains.

They got off at the first stop from the E train and Brian led Julie through the turnstiles and up the stairs onto the street, where the sun greeted them on the chilly November day.

"That's how everyone travels around here?" Julie asked.

Brian stepped to the street corner and waited for the light. "For the most part, yeah. There's the bus and taxis—some people have cars, but with

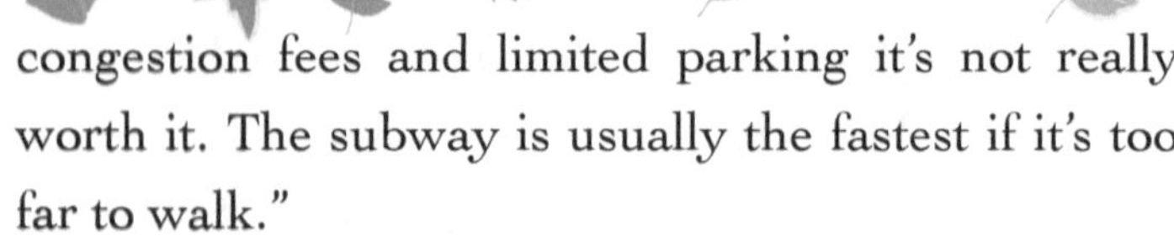

congestion fees and limited parking it's not really worth it. The subway is usually the fastest if it's too far to walk."

"Wow. This place really is a different world."

"You're not in the country anymore."

They crossed the street and Brian noticed the familiar surroundings of his Hells Kitchen neighborhood. The bodega on the corner that always had the best subs. The spot where he and his brother had been mugged when they were out late when he was sixteen.

Memories came flooding back to him the farther they walked.

Finally, they made it to his mother's apartment building. He used the key to unlock the door on the street, then led Julie up the steep steps to the third floor. Down a short hallway, he used a different key on apartment 3D and stepped inside.

The sounds of Mickey Mouse hit them and soon there were several faces looking at them. Both of Brian's brothers sat on the couch with their wives, and his nephews.

"Ma!" Jeffrey called into the kitchen. "Brian's home!"

She came out with an apron around her waist. "What is—" She stopped when she laid eyes on Brian. And behind him, Julie. "Who is that?"

Chapter Five
Thanksgiving
Julie

My heart thumped heavy in my chest as I felt everyone's eyes on me, scrutinizing me, trying to figure out who I was and why I was standing in their doorway.

Brian had failed to mention that his *entire family* would be waiting for us in his apartment. Then again, what did I expect? It was a holiday and he was clearly traveling for it.

Four adults and two kids were all sitting in the living room area, defined by the L-shaped couch that was situated in front of the TV. The two women were sitting on the edge of their seats, both leaned over toward the two little kids sitting on the floor in front of them. The

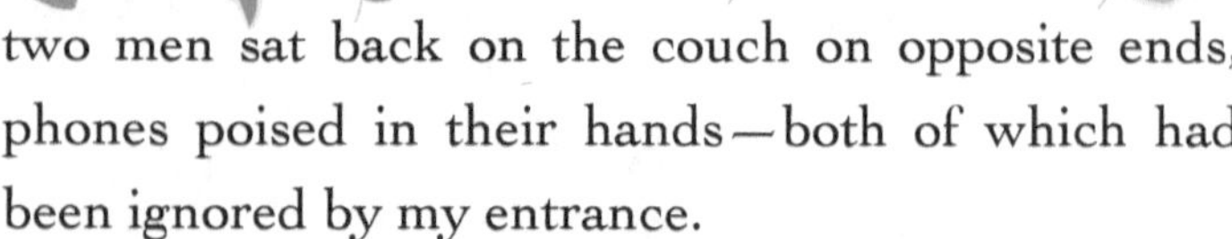

two men sat back on the couch on opposite ends, phones poised in their hands—both of which had been ignored by my entrance.

I shifted my weight on my feet awkwardly, waiting for Brian to break the silence in the room—the tension. There was no way in hell that I was going to be the one to talk first.

In the background, Mickey Mouse continued to prattle on. The kids, having grown bored of all the adults staring at each other, turned their attention back to the TV. The adults, meanwhile, were more enraptured by the deluge of gossip that would surely come after we left—or maybe just me.

Brian cleared his throat. "Um…everybody, this is Julie. She's a friend of mine that I just met on the bus. Julie, this is everyone." He began to point everyone out. "That's Jeffrey, my brother, and his wife, Tina. Then that's Mark, and his wife, Rebecca, and their kids, Brendan and Henry."

He looked up at his mother, still frozen in the doorway to the kitchen with a surprised look on her face. "Okay!" he said. "Well, I'm just going to drop off my things and then I'm going to show Julie around the city a bit." He started to step down the walkway created by the back of the couch and the kitchen wall, to the hallway around the corner, but his mother put her hand on his shoulder to stop him.

"Wait a minute, where's Kendra?" she asked.

I looked down at the floor. Kendra. Clearly he had meant to bring someone else. I idly wondered if this were one of those rom-com twists, where Brian was gay and had made up the name of a girlfriend to fool his family. But then, nothing about Brian seemed gay to me, so I pushed the thought aside.

"She didn't come," Brian said dismissively. "I'll be right back. This was just supposed to be a quick stop." He continued on down the hall with his mother following behind.

"Hey! Are you really ditching us like that?" Jeffrey called to him. "It's Thanksgiving! Family time!"

A door closing around the corner was all the response that the older brother got. I wondered if I should follow Brian in order to escape the scrutiny, but since his mother had followed him and they had closed the door—presumably to talk about Kendra— I decided it was better to stay put.

Still, I wanted to know what they were saying. About *Kendra*.

Was I jealous?

"Why don't you come and take a seat?" one of the wives asked me. I thought Brian had said her name was Rebecca. It had been a lot of information thrown at me at once. She scooted over, pulling one of the

kids up onto her lap from the floor.

Having no other alternative, I stepped into the living room area, which was separated only by the couch, and squeezed into a tight space between Jeffrey, Rebecca, and one of the boys, still in his pajamas.

After I sat, we all turned to the TV while Mickey continued to entertain the kids, even though I knew for a fact that not a single adult was paying attention to a word the animated mouse was saying.

I considered pulling out my phone and getting lost in it, but that would require me to lean into Jeffrey and pull my phone out of my back pocket, and it was too close to do that with someone I probably would never talk to again.

"So…where are you from?" Jeffrey asked me after a few silent moments.

"Um…out toward Buffalo," I said, grateful for some conversation. "A little town called Oakfield."

"Is that a suburb of Buffalo?" Rebecca asked.

I chuckled nervously. I couldn't imagine my small farm town being anything like the city of Buffalo—even Buffalo was nothing compared the metropolis of New York. "No, Oakfield is much further out than that. Probably about thirty, forty-five minutes to drive to Buffalo from Oakfield."

"Ah," she said politely while the rest of the them nodded in acknowledgement.

I wasn't sure if I was going to survive the awkwardness. How long did it take Brian to drop off his bag in his room? And I still needed to pee!

"What are you plans for the holiday?" Mark asked from the other end of the couch.

I hesitated. Brian said that New Yorkers typically stayed away from the highly-publicized events and spaces that non-New Yorkers loved. How naïve would I seem if I said I was here for the parade?

Then again, why did I care?

But I did.

"Um…I've, uh, I've never been to the city before and I thought my break from school would be the perfect opportunity to explore." It was a loose lie. I *was* on break and I *did* intend to explore the city. "Maybe try to get a glimpse of the parade." I needed to add one nugget of truth, in case Brian brought it up later.

But why did I care about protecting Brian from being caught in a lie?

Jeffrey made a face. "That's too many people for my liking. I'd rather just watch it on TV."

Beside me, Rebecca shot him a warning glare across me that I pretended not to notice.

"You think it'll be that crowded?" I asked

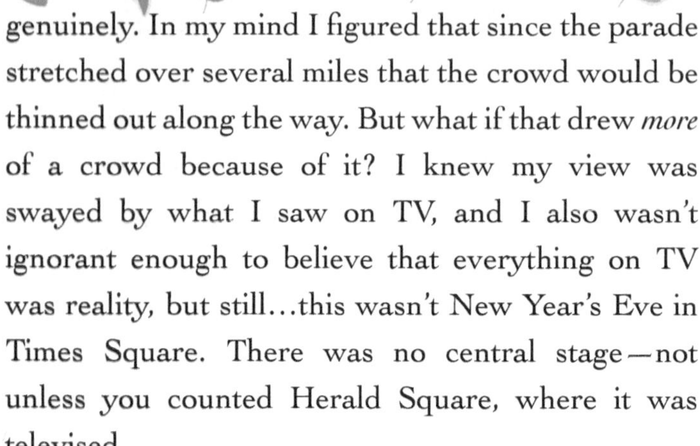

genuinely. In my mind I figured that since the parade stretched over several miles that the crowd would be thinned out along the way. But what if that drew *more* of a crowd because of it? I knew my view was swayed by what I saw on TV, and I also wasn't ignorant enough to believe that everything on TV was reality, but still…this wasn't New Year's Eve in Times Square. There was no central stage—not unless you counted Herald Square, where it was televised.

"Oh yeah," Mark chimed in. "I'm sure there's a ton of security, but that's still a lot of people."

Security. Another reminder that I hadn't thought this through. Maybe Brian was right. Maybe we were risking arrest by doing this.

I was beginning to regret accepting the dare. Again. How had I allowed myself to be so easily manipulated?

Because of Eric. He was a giant teddy bear and I wanted to be wrapped up in his arms. Sure, he *did* act like a wild boy most of the time but I was sure he'd be different one-on-one. I was sure he'd be different toward a girlfriend. If he'd ever consider me in that way.

"Well," I said, forcing a smile onto my face, "we'll just have to see how close we can get."

Tina cocked an eyebrow. "We? As in, you and Brian?"

My smile began to fade as I understood the implication. "Yeah. He's offered to show me around."

Jeffrey and Mark both turned and smiled at one another, then burst out laughing.

Rebecca swatted her husband on the leg, then turned to me. "I'm sorry about them."

Of course, I knew what they were thinking. They were insinuating that Brian and I were together. Which we weren't. I was pining after Eric while Brian had something going on with Kendra.

Or *not* going on with her. Whatever the deal was. I didn't care.

Why would I care about Brian's relationship status?

Why *did* I care about Brian's relationship status?

"That sounds like fun," Rebecca added.

"So…are you two…?" Tina started.

I shook my head. "No! No. We're just—we just met. On the bus." I clamped my mouth shut from saying anything else. The more I said, the more it made me sound like a hooker picking up men at the bus stop.

"Oh okay," Rebecca said with a smile. "That's nice of him, then."

"Yeah, it is," I said with a nod.

Nobody said anything further. We all turned back to Mickey Mouse and gave the computer animated cartoon our full attention. Well, everyone except me, whose mind was racing with doubt, worry, and a little bit of lust.

Chapter Six
Thanksgiving
Brian

When Brian stepped into the guest room—his old bedroom—he was surprised to see that the bed had already been slept in. Bags were lined up on the dresser and an air mattress lay on the floor.

The surprise faded quickly. Of course. Jeffrey and Rebecca and the kids must've spent the night in here instead of coming down this morning from Tarrytown. He wondered if Mark and Tina had spent the night, too or if they rode the train in at the crack of dawn. Regardless, they would be staying here tonight. Rebecca, Tina, and Brian's mother always went Black Friday shopping in the city every year.

"Brian," his mother said softly from behind him. She

closed the door so the two of them were alone.

"What?" he snapped. He found a flat surface to set his bag and began to search for the things that could've potentially leaked all over the inside—toothpaste, aftershave, face wash. That was just what he needed—no clothes to wear on his sudden move back home.

He had no idea where he'd be sleeping. Apparently his mother had forgotten that this used to be his room and had given it away so quickly to her other son. Her *golden* son. The one who had given her grandchildren. As if that wasn't ever a possibility for Brian himself.

Taking a deep breath, he shifted his anger away from his family. It wasn't their fault his life had crumbled to pieces. That had been his doing all on his own. Him and his stupid ignorance and trust in a woman who took advantage of that.

And it only made sense that this room would be the one Jeffrey and his family took. He and Brian *had* shared it growing up. It had only become solely Brian's when Jeffrey went away to college.

"Welcome home," his mother finally said. She rubbed his shoulder and he wrapped his arm around her in a sideway hug. "I'm so happy to see you."

"Thanks." He pulled out the toothpaste and

mouthwash from his bag, then rifled through for his aftershave. Each of the items were in plastic bags, but he had had more than one accident with travel messes before that he didn't want to take any chances. Besides, it helped focus his attention on something other than his mother. And his anger.

"Who is that girl?" his mother asked.

Brian let out a deep breath. He hadn't expected all of this. Another reason for his annoyance. "Her name is Julie."

Out of the corner of his eye, he saw his mother nod slowly. "And where is Kendra?"

"Back in Canada."

"She didn't want to come for American Thanksgiving?"

He turned toward her. "It's a long story, Mom."

"Is Julie your new girlfriend?"

"What!" he blurted. The idea had never crossed his mind. He had only just met her twelve hours before. But then, she had been easy to talk to. And even though she was insufferable at times, she did make him laugh. And when he caught her on the subway, he had noticed just how beautiful her she was.

He shook his head. "No, Mom. She's just someone I met on the bus. She's never been to the city before and I told her I'd show her around." He

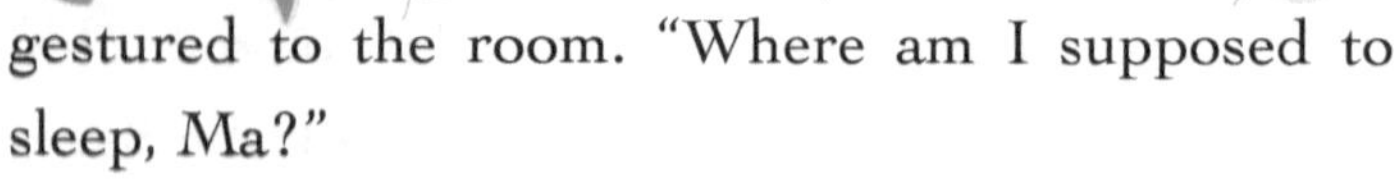

gestured to the room. "Where am I supposed to sleep, Ma?"

His mother's eyes widened, as if the thought had just occurred to her. "Oh! I guess there isn't enough room in here for everyone. You could sleep on the couch, unless you wanted to bunk with me."

Brian made a face. "I'm not going to share a room with my *mother*. I'm a grown adult." That was just what he needed on his plummet down to rock bottom. To wind up sharing a bed with his mother on a holiday while everyone else in his life had someone else. "The couch will be fine."

She put up her hands in surrender. "Okay, okay. It was just a suggestion. I need to get back to the kitchen so everything is ready in time. Are you sure you're okay?"

"I'm fine," he said, then added as a distraction, "Is anyone helping you?" He didn't want his mother slaving away in the kitchen all day while he gallivanted around town with a girl he had just met in order to avoid the aftershocks of his imploding life, all while his brothers and their wives sat around watching TV all day. It wasn't fair. Brian would ditch Julie in a heartbeat if it meant keeping his mother from preparing the whole feast herself.

"Yes, the girls have already volunteered. It's a little early yet to get too busy with anything. I'm just working on the dessert so it can bake before I put the turkey in." She cupped his face in her hands and smiled at him. "Don't worry about me. Go and have fun with your…friend." Her face seemed to sour a little.

"What's the matter?"

She took a deep breath and pulled away. "It's just that, if you haven't broken up with Kendra yet, then it's wrong for you to be starting up anything with anyone else. I didn't raise you like that."

Brian was quiet. His mother had the wrong impression of Julie. He debated whether he should dive into the long story then, but thought about how long that would take. How much his mother would want to talk about it. How it might ruin her Thanksgiving to know that one of her sons was moving backwards in life. How word might spread to his brothers and, if Brian wasn't going to tell them himself, they would probably spend the weekend whispering and speculating about where Kendra was and why she wasn't there celebrating with them.

He suddenly felt very overwhelmed. The rush of emotions from the previous day, the long travel, being unexpectedly greeted by his entire family, having his bedroom taken over, and having Julie waiting for him out in the living room where his brothers might be asking her anything…it was all becoming too much. Not to mention the expectations of the holiday and everything with Kendra and Julie and—

He needed to get out.

"I'm not cheating on Kendra," he said finally. "Please don't pry into my life anymore. I'll tell you when I'm ready." He grabbed his wallet from the dresser and brushed past his mother.

It wasn't fair. What happened to him. How he found out. Where he was now. What he had said to his mother.

His response had been harsh. He would need to apologize later for it. But at the moment, he just needed to escape.

Out in the living room again, everyone's attention snapped to him as soon as he stepped out of the bedroom. With the way they each craned their necks in an uncomfortable position told him that they had each been anxiously waiting for him to emerge. So they could witness any more gossip about what was happening. Two married couples living vicariously through him. As if his life was so great.

"There he is!" Jeffrey called out. An attempt to soften the tension. "Come say hi! How've you been, little brother?"

Brian ignored him—ignored them all—and locked eyes with Julie, who gave him a look that begged for relief from the awkward entrapment she found herself in.

"You ready?" he asked.

She shot up out of her seat and stepped to the door.

"Brian, you're really just going to leave without saying anything to us?" Mark asked. He upturned his hand and scrunched up his face, as if Brian's actions revolted him. His arm was slung over the back of the couch, behind Tina, and he craned his neck sideways to face Brian.

"You just got here," Rebecca said. "The kids have been talking about you."

"Let's go," he said to Julie, then stepped around her to open the door.

Julie turned to his family and waved. "It was nice meeting you all. If I don't see you again, I hope you have a nice Thanksgiving."

"You too, sweetie," Tina said with a smile.

Rebecca offered a polite smile of her own, but her face read confusion. Jeffrey and Mark both looked at each other and shook their heads.

Out in the hall, with the door shut behind them, Brian started to feel like he could breathe again. A little.

"Your family is nice," Julie said as they walked down the hall toward the stairs.

"Yep, they're all just peaches, aren't they?" he grumbled.

"Do you—" she started as they descended the stairs, but stopped herself from finishing.

At the bottom of the staircase, Brian paused by the mail slots. "Do I *what*?"

She diverted her eyes, clearly second-guessing what she was really going to ask. "Do you know of a place nearby where I can stop and pee?"

"Oh. Right. Sorry." He had forgotten she had said she needed to do that. And, on second thought, he had forgotten that *he* needed to take care of the same business. "Yeah, there's a Starbucks around the corner. We can get some coffee before we leave, too. My treat." He felt bad for putting her through that whole ordeal with his family.

And it wasn't like he was even mad at his family. He just wasn't ready to deal with them yet and their inevitable questions.

Guess he owed the whole family an apology. And one to Julie. Coffee was a place to start, though.

He pulled the door open and nodded for her to head out toward the street. "Come on. We don't have a lot of time if you want to get in that parade."

Chapter Seven
Thanksgiving
Julie

With Starbucks coffee in hand, I felt like a true New Yorker. My phone was filling up fast with photos and short videos of different things I'd seen so far. Passing taxi cabs, the busy sidewalks, the staircase leading down to the subway. Everywhere I turned, inspiration struck.

I was grateful I had only brought my large purse. Then I could feel less like a tourist and more like a New Yorker. Although, the pace that Brian walked at as he marched down the street was much faster than I was used to.

Music greeted us as we descended the steps at the 50th Street subway station. Jazzy, soulful, and smooth.

The saxophone cut through the noise of the city, providing a melody to the mundane.

"What is that?" I asked Brian.

He shrugged. "Probably someone playing their saxophone for money."

My eyes widened. This truly was a full New York experience! I had always wanted to see one of these performers in person. And the music sounded incredible.

At the gate in the subway station, Brian again stepped through the emergency exit and allowed me to pass through with him. I had barely registered the smelly breeze on my face before I started searching around for the source of the music.

As we came upon the platform, though, I saw him. A black man sat in a small camping chair with his saxophone case opened in front of him with a few bills in it. He had his eyes closed and played with all of his heart and soul.

Immediately, I pulled out my phone and went live, recording the trills. As each person began to populate on my live, the comments began to pour in.

BEAUTIFUL!

ARE YOU IN NEW YORK?

I noticed that the picture quality on my phone was lagging since we were underground. Or maybe it was the crowd of people around us, all with their own phones and other devices, trying to connect to the same limited wireless networks. We were all so connected. All the time.

I ended the Live, then went to open my camera app to record a video instead, but too many people were in my way.

Beside me, I heard Brian's voice and felt him tug on my arm a little. "Come on, or we'll miss our train."

With a sigh of disappointment, I turned and followed him to the right platform and waited. We found a spot away from the bulk of the crowd. I had learned by now that that meant our possibility of getting on a quieter train was higher, but not always.

"You need to cool it with the pictures and the videos and all the things with the phone," he said.

"But this might be my only trip to New York!" I said. "I need to savor the memories."

"You need to protect yourself from being an easy target."

"Easy target for what?" I asked. "Is Detective Benson going to come in here to solve a crime?" Okay, maybe my knowledge of New York City had been limited to pop culture. *Law & Order: SVU* among my obsessions.

"No, but you could be the victim of a pickpocket," he said.

"Oh no. I'll watch out for…*pickpockets*," I deadpanned.

"I'm serious. All it takes it someone with a blade to slice through that purse of yours and grab your wallet. Or maybe they can slip their hand in and grab it. Think about it, your credit cards, your ID, your home address—all of it would be open to whoever steals your cards."

I looked at him, stubbornly standing my ground. "How often does that really happen?"

"Often enough. Especially to people who aren't careful."

"So, what? Am I not supposed to walk with a bag?"

"No, but you should be more mindful of your surroundings. Look at the way you sling your bag behind you like you don't have a care in the world. You have no idea who is reaching in there—or *slipping* something in there."

I shifted my purse to my front, suddenly realizing Brian's concerns. "Slipping something like *what* in my bag?"

He shrugged. "Could be anything. Do you really want to find out?"

I sighed, feeling the magic of New York slowly begin to slip away. Still, I tried to hold on to what was left.

"And if you lose yourself in your phone every few minutes, some people will use that distraction to their advantage," he went on.

"Well, it's a good thing I have you, then," I murmured, not willing to give him the win outwardly. "But can you relax a little and enjoy the holiday? It's Thanksgiving! Our only obligations today is at the end of the day. And that's to stuff our faces."

Brian looked away.

"And since I'm away from home, when you will be stuffing your face with turkey, I'll probably be on a bus somewhere on my way back to Oakfield, uploading and documenting this spontaneous trip to the Big Apple on all my social media accounts."

His stony exterior crumbled as he barked out a

laugh. "People who live in the city don't call it that."

"Sure they do," I countered. "I read. In a lot of articles about New York City they call it the Big Apple. And, I should point out, those articles are usually written by people who *live* here."

Brian rolled his eyes. "Okay, so they do call it that, but that's more so they're not being repetitive in an article about the city. They don't use it in everyday conversation."

Wind rose up from down the tunnel as another train came up to the platform with a screech of brakes. My hair blew over my shoulders behind me as I turned to face the train, resisting the urge to bring up my phone and snap a picture. It would've been a good shot. Probably would've gotten a lot of likes.

When the train finally stopped with a hiss, the doors opened…and nobody stepped out.

"Empty car?" I asked Brian.

"Another rule of being a New Yorker," Brian said as we stepped on, "always be skeptical of an empty subway car. There's probably a reason it's empty." He looked around once we got on. "In this case, this one is empty because it's a holiday. Not as many people traveling on the subway."

I started to take a seat, but Brian caught my arm and kept me on my feet.

"What?"

"Our stop isn't that far," he said. "And, I anticipate it getting more crowded the further uptown we go. The closer to the parade. We don't want to be stuck on the wrong side of the train and can't get out at our stop."

I straightened up and fixed the strap on my purse, making sure the bulk of it was in front of me. "Oh. Okay."

He smiled. "You have a lot to learn if you want to pass as a New Yorker."

"I *am* a New Yorker," I declared. "Just not a city-dwelling New Yorker." The train lurched to a start. Luckily, this time, I was prepared and grasped the pole in the center of the train, just under Brian's own hand.

Another roll of his eyes. "You live Upstate."

"Upstate as in the *majority* of the state?" I tapped my chin and looked up and over to the side. "Hmm...I don't know about that. By my standards, Upstate is the Adirondacks area. You know, the *upper* part of the *whole* state."

"Okay, but—"

I put up my hand to stop him. No matter what his argument was, it would be skewed to some New York City-centered idea. "Let's just agree to disagree about our views of New York State."

"At the risk of firing up another unsolvable debate, can I ask you where you'd consider yourself from, if not Upstate?"

"*Western* New York."

He shrugged. "That's splitting hairs a bit."

I scrunched up my face and looked up at him. "Oh, so I can just say that you live in Brooklyn because it's *basically* the same thing as Manhattan, right?"

He cocked an eyebrow. "Touché. I guess that everyone has their own preconceived notions about places where they don't live."

The robotic recorded voice announced the 79th Street stop and Brian moved toward the doors.

"This is our stop." He stood close and as soon as the doors hissed and opened, he stepped out. I hurried after him, grateful to not get caught up in the people clambering to get on as fast as they could.

Up on the street, Brian rushed to the crosswalk and waved me on. "Come on! We can get across before the light changes!"

I saw fifteen seconds left on the timer across the street — Broadway, according to the street sign — and didn't think that we would make it in time, but Brian was determined. I broke out into a jog to keep up with him.

The timer finished and the orange hand began to

flash, indicating that the signal was about to change. We stepped onto the sidewalk on the other side just as the orange hand stopped flashing and remained solid. Seconds later, cars whizzed by behind us as their light changed to green.

Even though we were safely across the street, there was no period of rest. I had to pump my legs to keep up with Brian's quick pace.

"Would you slow down?" I groaned as I jogged to catch up.

"Not if you want to make it in time," he said. "The parade is starting soon."

"Okay, but…" My voice trailed off. I didn't really have a good rebuttal to his statement. He was, after all, doing this for me. Or was there another reason for him helping a stranger?

I pushed thoughts of any kind of romantic attraction away—my sights were set on Eric who, surprisingly, hadn't even texted yet to check in. Although, truth be told, he was probably still passed out from the wild Thanksgiving Eve night.

How different our lives had become in the last twelve hours. I thought about sending him a text with a picture when I got a chance—if I ever got a chance.

The only ones who had texted so far were my brother, who simply typed:

MOM IS PISSED. WHERE ARE YOU?

I hadn't had time to type out a reply to him. Especially when my mother sent me a vicious text shortly afterwards, berating me for "disappearing" on her. As if she actually cared where I was.

Another ignore.

Shifting back to Brian, I thought about how tense his mother's apartment had been. He had been so desperate to get out of there. Maybe that was why he was so devoted to this random dare. According to him on the bus, the whole idea was stupid. And yet here he was.

So why was he helping me?

We risked being run down again when we crossed the next street. Breathless now, I caught back up with Brian's pace, which began to slow as we approached yet another intersection.

"How do you even know where the parade starts?" I asked him, hoping the conversation would slow him down.

He shrugged. "I just do."

We crossed the intersection and worked our way around the block. From the signs I scanned as we passed, it was the American Museum of Natural History—another place that looked cool. I wished we had time to stop. Then again, they were probably closed for Thanksgiving.

The murmur of a crowd became louder the closer we got to the park — Central Park — which was in full bloom with all the different colors of the fall leaves. It was beautiful.

I pulled out my phone and snapped a picture, then began to record a video. The people around this area were here for the parade. Tourists themselves, even if they were from New York City. Chances were, none of them were pickpockets like Brian feared. Or worse.

Brian pressed on, oblivious to the fact that I had slowed. He turned to say something to me, then saw that I wasn't there and spun around.

"What are you doing? Come on!"

I ended the video, slipped the phone in my pocket, then raced after him. "I couldn't resist the shot."

"You're going to have to focus if you want to get in the parade," he said. "Now, start looking around for costumed characters. Maybe we can persuade them to trade out their outfits with us so we can get on one of the floats."

The street running alongside the park had been closed off and there was a crowd forming in front of the museum, held back by metal barricades.

I reached for Brian's arm as he meandered

through the crowd to the barricade. He didn't seem to pay any attention to the number of people he was bumping into or the curses tossed his way.

"We have to get over there." Brian pointed across the street to the park, where there were trailers parked along the road that usually ran through the center of the park, but had been closed off for the occasion.

"Um, Brian, we can't just take over a costumed character," I reminded him. "My friends need to see my face on the parade."

The original dare had seemed like a lifetime ago. My brain was foggy from little sleep on the bus and having such a long day. And, of course, the alcohol the night before didn't help matters at all.

"It's a start, okay? Either way, we need to find a way over there."

The parade was beginning to line up on the street. People were dressed in costumes from Broadway musicals, others were dressed up as if it were only ten degrees outside when the reality was a cool but comfortable forty-five and sunny.

Some of the marching bands were practicing. Parade directors were walking at a frenzied pace up and down the street, pointing and gesturing wildly as they directed the performers. Security guards traveled in a lazy gait, eyes scanning back and forth, hoping that only their presence would be enough to deter any nuisances.

"Follow me," Brian told me and began to lead me along the barricade.

My hand was still locked firmly against his arm—which was much firmer than I had expected, underneath his jacket—and I followed him without question.

"Excuse me," Brian murmured. "Coming through. Just passing by."

More groans and looks of disgust came our way as we stepped into people's personal spaces, threatening to impede on their hard-fought view of the parade.

One man—larger even than Eric—refused to budge. When Brian tried to squeeze by, the man put his hand on the barricade and glared down at us. "Back off."

"We just need to get by," Brian said.

The man turned on him, his face turning angry. Sensing a confrontation none of us wanted, I tugged on Brian's arm and led him deeper into the crowd, escaping back onto the sidewalk where the crowd was thinner.

"I was hoping to stay closer to the fence so that we could find a spot in it to walk through," he said.

"That guy looked like he was going to punch you in the face."

"He wouldn't have hit me. Not with all those people."

"You don't know that. Besides, we'll piss off less people if we find a break in the barricade from back here."

Brian waved me forward. "Lead the way, then."

"Come on!" I grabbed his hand and led him around the crowd, only realizing after I'd taken several steps that I had so brazenly claimed ownership of him—even if temporarily.

The barricades extended all the way down the street, but the crowd thinned the farther away from the start of the parade. We made our way to a point in the barricades where two of the fence pieces were linked together.

"Here," Brian said as he began to lift the one so that we could slide through.

"Sir, you can't come in here," a firm voice said. It had an accent, but I couldn't quite place it. Not yet. Not with so few words spoken.

We looked over and saw a large man in a white security guard uniform. He met Brian's eyes, then looked down at his hands on the portable fencing.

The security guard walked over. Officer Quick, according to the name tag on his uniform. It made me wonder if it was one of those divine intervention things. Like he wouldn't have become a security guard if his last name had been Slow or Turtle.

The guard walked over and eyed him. "Don't do something you'll regret, son."

There it was. The southern drawl took me by surprise. Not something I had ever expected to hear in New York City. Guess New York truly was a melting pot of all different cultures and backgrounds.

"We just want to get over to the park," Brian lied. "We don't want to have to go all the way up the street just to come back down."

"I'll save you the trouble." Officer Quick hoisted up his belt under his large belly. "This whole area is closed off to the public, on account of the parade. You're not looking to cause trouble, are ya?"

"No, sir," Brian said. "I just—we're just trying to go for a nice walk in the park. I completely forgot that the parade was today."

Quick narrowed his eyes. "You forgot the Thanksgiving Day Parade was on Thanksgiving Day?" he asked, although it came out more like *Thanksgivun*.

"Look, I don't see the harm in us cutting through," Brian pleaded. "You can even escort us if it'll make you feel better."

He shook his head. "No can do, son. Not while my job is on the line. No thank you, sir-ee."

"But—"

I put a hand on Brian's shoulder and stepped in front of him, pulling out my phone. "Officer," I said with a flirty smile. "I'm sorry about this terrible mix-up. Can I please get a selfie with you? I just so admire your profession—all lines of law enforcement deserve to be respected. And certainly someone so ruggedly handsome as yourself."

Somebody should've given me an Oscar for my acting skills. Officer Quick was a far cry from Eric. And even Brian. Of course, Brian and Quick weren't even in the same league. Neither were Eric and Brian. Quick and Eric were both large men, but Eric was more stocky than fat, with the underlying confidence that made him attractive.

Brian was…well, Brian was more boy-next-door. Someone who snuck up on you when you least expected them to. Someone who had been there, standing by, quietly handsome all along.

But why was I considering Brian's looks? I was doing all of this for Eric. Maybe I'd send him the selfie with Quick and make a comment about their looks. Something to push us further out of the friend zone.

Officer Quick warmed at my charm. "Oh, yes ma'am. Anything for a pretty lady."

He leaned in beside me until our shoulders touched. I raised my phone and snapped several pictures.

"Look at that! I'll post it online and use the hashtag #respectlawenforcement. That way you'll be able to find it."

He shook his head. "I'm not one for all that internet business, ma'am." Or, as he put it, *inner-net bid-ness*.

"Well, then, it'll be out there for the world to see regardless," I said. "Thank you." Glancing over, I saw that the fence was firmly in place still.

Couldn't Brian pick up on the fact that I was creating a diversion?

"I love the strong sexy type," I told the officer, changing tactics a bit. "Can I take a picture from behind?"

Officer Quick's demeanor soured. "Now, wait a minute—"

"Can't talk, gotta go!" Brian grabbed my hand and yanked me away from the guard. Further down, the barricade was being moved for an outgoing car.

We booked it and made it through the barricades in time, with the guards who had opened it calling out to us.

"Hey! This is a closed area! We need to see ID!"

We ignored them and darted by. Meanwhile, Officer Quick was running after us with a speed that was surprisingly fast for someone with his bulk. Maybe there was something to his name after all.

Across the street, several other guards took notice and tried to block our path, but Brian led us toward the stone fence separating the park from the road.

I prepared to jump over the fence and surprised myself at how easily I hopped over it. We ran down a paved sidewalk that took us down a hill, then darted around into a parking lot that was hidden among the trees and the hills. I wouldn't have even seen it if Brian hadn't pulled me in.

Then, with a jerk, he yanked me to the ground and held me close as we huddled in the fallen leaves, sandwiched between what felt like the roots of a tree and the stone wall lining the walking path in the park.

My back was pressed against Brian's chest. More noticeably, our lower regions were pressed together as well. I tried to shift so that we were sitting side-by-side, but that caused the leaves to crunch and he tightened his arms around me.

"Shh," he murmured right against my ear.

I supposed there were worse people I could've been been stuck to. Brian's arms *did* seem to fit so perfectly around—

Heavy boots sounded on the walkway, just on the other side of the fence. I sunk deeper into Brian, hoping the guards wouldn't see us. Disobeying a direct order from a security guard spoke of trouble — if there was a temporary city order issued, then we could potentially be facing charges with the police.

My heart thumped heavy in my chest and I suddenly felt hot in my winter coat — the running and being pressed against Brian didn't help matters any.

Finally, the boots passed on and Brian released his hold on me. I slid into a space beside him, leaves rustling with the movement, then looked over at him with terror. Running away from security guards and disobeying a direct order? Things were getting real.

Brian, meanwhile, was smiling. Then, he broke into laughter. It was infectious and I started laughing, too, boosted by the absurdity of what had just happened. Not even five minutes ago we were standing on the sidewalk trying to get through with a whole crowd of other onlookers, and then we were racing away from an overweight security guard — who I had just pretended to flirt with — and ended up hiding in the weeds.

Brian's laughs faded as we began to rise, only then realizing that our hands had become interlocked again.

Chapter Eight
Thanksgiving
Julie

The parade had started. The floats had been steadily moving out of the park. Any other workers who were joining the parade were getting in line, ready for their float to pull away. It was going to be impossible to get on one, and I was beginning to accept that the dare was not going to be accomplished.

Brian, meanwhile, seemed undeterred. He was already making his way down the walkway, making sure to lead us to a different one than the ones where the guards had chased us.

"What are you doing?" I motioned to the floats getting into formation down on the street that cut through the park. "They're all leaving, or about to."

"I know," Brian said. He was several feet ahead of me, walking with a purpose—marching, really. It was the theme of the morning, wasn't it?

The real question was: when had this become so important to him? Hours ago, he had been teasing me for even dreaming of attempting something like this. Now, he seemed more determined than I was.

We crossed the pedestrian bridge over 79th Street, then followed the meandering paths deeper into the park.

"Where are we going?" I asked.

"This way."

"Are you mad at me?"

"No."

"Okay, well, the short responses aren't making me feel warm and fuzzy." I wondered if this had to do with how close we were. It had certainly been weird. Not something I ever expected to happen with a stranger. But Brian was fast becoming someone who *wasn't* a stranger. And that was an odd feeling, considering twenty-four hours ago I didn't know the man even existed.

Still, I couldn't help but think back to how he so confidently took my hand. How I so easily followed him. How nice it felt to feel his body against mine. How easy it was to laugh with him.

To talk with him. Even when he frustrated me — *especially* when he frustrated me.

My phone buzzed and I stopped to look at who the text was from. My step-dad. All the text read was:

WHERE ARE YOU?

Randy and I had had a decent relationship, despite the fact that he had grown to hate my mother throughout their marriage. We were cordial, polite, but altogether disinterested in one another beyond that. Even though the text had come from Randy, I knew my mother was behind it. So I tucked my phone back in my pocket.

I jogged to catch up to Brian, who had been getting further and further away from me.

"So what are we doing then?" My eyes glanced over at the lake to my left. Okay, so it was probably a pond. A very large pond. But this was the place where so many photos online had been taken. Edited heavily, of course, but still. This was the origin point.

Craning my neck to the right, I could see the iconic apartment buildings that lined the park poking up through the fall leaves. I pulled out my phone and snapped a picture. Then turned and admired the tree-lined path we had just come down and snapped another picture. I turned so my back was to the lake and raised my phone to take a selfie in front of it, but a call came through before I could snap the pic.

My mother.

I hesitated, feeling every muscle in my body tense up. My eyes glanced over to Brian, who had noticed that I had stopped and turned back to look at me. He was about twenty feet ahead. Definitely out of earshot of anything that would spew between me and my mother.

I turned back to my phone. It said it was just about eight o'clock. And apparently my mother had *just* found out that I wasn't actually home.

Mother of the year.

Ignoring texts was one thing, but I knew that if I didn't answer the phone call, the wrath would be even worse when I got home. And since I didn't have a solid plan on how I was *getting* home, I slid the bottom of my phone and answered.

"Hello?"

"Julie Marie Griffiths, where the *hell* are you?" my mother barked on the other end.

Her voice seemed to rip me right out of such a peaceful setting, completely disrupting the tranquility of the park.

"I've been worried sick!" she added as her voice calmed.

Lie.

I knew my mother wasn't worried sick. She wanted to know where I was because she needed to have control over me. And this anger was her suddenly realizing that she *didn't* have control. As if she ever did.

"I, uh…I took an impromptu trip." I tried to act casual, even as Brian came back over to me. I didn't want him to hear my conversation, so I turned away and took a few steps in the opposite direction, my body language telling him to give me some space. I only caught a glimpse of his face, but he looked dejected.

I wasn't the best version of myself when my mother was around.

"An impromptu trip?" she asked with disgust. "You're on a friggin' vacation while I'm slaving away in this kitchen and you couldn't even *tell* me you weren't going to be here for dinner? You selfish bitch."

"Okay, I should've told you," I admitted, sidestepping her comment.

"Where are you?"

"New York."

There was a pause, then, "Don't get smart with me. Where *are* you?"

She misunderstood, and correcting her would

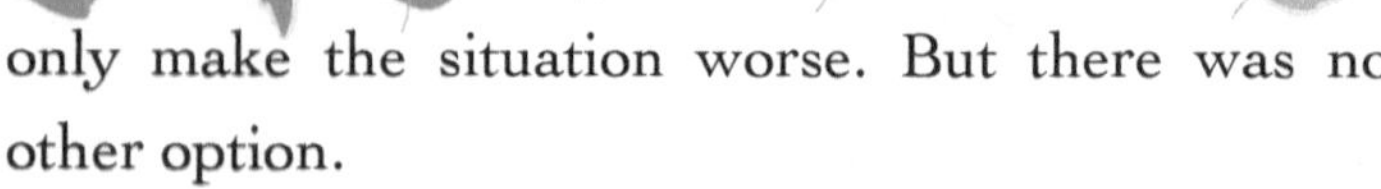

only make the situation worse. But there was no other option.

"New York *City*."

My mother scoffed on the other end. "You're probably there to watch that stupid parade you're always talking about every year. It's not enough for you to lay around and watch it on TV all morning every year while I'm trying to get dinner ready, now you just up and disappear to go see it without one word to me."

I kicked myself for not being a better person. Common courtesy would be to tell someone that you weren't going to be home for dinner, as was expected. I hadn't done that.

But I also knew my mother. Dinner was just an excuse to yell. She liked to yell. She didn't know how to be happy. And, if I had learned one thing growing up with her, it was that nothing I did—or anyone did—would ever make her happy.

Brian had taken a seat on a park bench several feet away. His arms stretched out along the back of it, his legs sprawled in front of him while he watched the sunlight shining through the many colors of the trees. The branches above him created a canopy over the path, while the gentle breeze sent a few leaves dropping to the ground, almost like snowfall.

What a difference from whatever ugly place my mother had taken me with a simple phone call.

I resisted the urge to apologize to my mother—a defense mechanism to keep the peace that I would spend the rest of my adult life unlearning—and waited for her to decide the conversation was over.

"Well," my mother finally said, "if you want to be a selfish little girl who is just like every other bimbo in that overbuilt city, then you can just stay there."

The phone beeped twice in my ear, signaling the call had been ended.

Without even realizing it, my shoulders slumped and I felt a heaviness come over my body that hadn't been there before the call. I hated that my mother had that kind of power over me and my emotions. Leaving for college had been the saving grace that I had been looking for, but after nearly four years spending most of my time away from home, it still wasn't enough to completely escape her clutches.

My mother knew my time with her was coming to an end. And as a woman who needed to control everything in her life, she hated it. That was exactly why I needed to get out of my mother's house as quickly as possible. I just wished I had a guarantee that after graduation, I would be able to leave right away. But in this economy, nothing was a guarantee.

Brian noticed that my call had ended and was already walking toward me by the time I turned back to him.

"Everything okay?" he asked.

My thumb hovered over my mother's number on my phone, debating whether I should call her back and apologize. I had at least another six months with the woman. I needed to keep the peace until then. And after graduation? Who knew?

But for the moment, I was in a beautiful park in a big city with a very sweet man who was helping me achieve something I'd always wanted to do.

I needed to forget my mother and enjoy the moment.

"Yeah," I said with a nod, not meeting Brian's gaze. "Everything's fine."

He was quiet for several seconds. I could almost feel his eyes on me. Finally, he said, "Okay, well, I was thinking that if we started heading down along the park and met up with the parade down the block…"

His voice faded from my consciousness as my phone buzzed with a text. It was Eric.

My heart fluttered at the excitement of him

texting me individually. Usually when we texted it was part of a group. And actually, when our friend group first started texting, the boys had played a joke on us and refused to tell us whose numbers were whose, leaving the girls left to decipher and discuss which number belonged to which person. The boys thought it was hysterical. The girls thought it was mildly amusing. Now, I see that it was kind of childish.

> JULES! ARE YOU ACTUALLY IN NYC OR ARE YOU JUST LAYING LOW AT HOME? 😂 😂 😂

Automatically, my fingers tapped the screen as I attached the selfie I had just taken in front of the lake and then typed out a reply. Out of the corner of my eye, I saw Brian had wandered off again. I had completely ignored him. When he was trying to help *me*.

Maybe my mother was right. Maybe I was selfish.

My eyes darted back and forth between my phone and Brian. Eric's last text to me was on my birthday, but he couldn't wish me a happy birthday in the regular way, he had to make a joke out of it.

What had followed was a text from me, desperately trying to engage in a conversation with him that failed to go anywhere.

My birthday was four months ago. He hadn't texted me since then.

Idly, I wondered what Brian would've done for my birthday. I'm sure he would've sent a text. I'm sure he would've come to a party if I had had one. I'm sure he would've made sure I had had a good day.

Eric was the type of person who partied so hard the night before Thanksgiving that he slept through most of the holiday, only to go back out the next night. Brian, on the other hand, was the type of person who would help a complete stranger achieve a wildly crazy dream. And after all of that, he was still planning on going home to spend the holiday with his family, even though there was definitely a lot of awkward tension going on—for whatever reason. Even through all of that, family was still most important to him.

I've always wanted a family. A good family. One

with unconditional love. One who still wanted you with them even when things were hard. Not a perfect family, but a loving one.

Eric pressured me into abandoning my—albeit sad—Thanksgiving plans for a dare that he wasn't even accompanying me on. And all for what? A few laughs at the hometown bar that he frequented every weekend, and probably would continue to for the rest of his life?

And then there was Brian.

I smiled and walked over to him. He was looking back to the parking lot where the parade floats were getting in line to file out onto the street. The people manning the ones at the end of the parade were still sitting comfortably, waiting for the first half of the parade to start so that they could get in line.

Brian pointed to Santa's sleigh, which was always the end of the parade. He smiled at me. "I think I have a plan."

Chapter Nine
Thanksgiving
Brian

"**A**re you planning on having us sneak onto Santa's sleigh?" Julie asked with a smirk.

Brian raised his eyebrows and cocked his head to the side, his attention still focused on the parking lot across 79th Street in the park. "I thought about that, but Santa is the culminating event of the whole parade. He's a highly televised—and photographed—part of the whole thing. If we traded places with Santa and Mrs. Claus, we would be called out."

The unspoken truth was made aware for the both of them: sneaking on Santa's sleigh would bring a higher risk of being arrested.

"What if we just snuck in the back of the sleigh?"

Julie suggested. "Maybe then we could just poke our heads out and wave to get noticed in a few pictures, but hide and escape before anyone can catch us."

Brian shook his head. "I think we would be under arrest before the parade even finished. They would be *looking* for us—and they'd have the photographs to remind them what we looked like. There's no way we'd be able to escape easily. And then think of the press."

"Well, that'd be one way to prove I was there," she muttered.

"But would it be worth it?"

She crossed her arms. "So what do you suggest we do?"

He pointed, although with the distance it was hard to tell exactly what he was pointing at. "Look at all those trailers sitting there, waiting for the parade to end before they're carted off."

Down in the parking lot, there were remnants of the hubbub of organized chaos that had been there not even fifteen minutes ago. While most of the people had cleared out, there were still some stragglers amongst the parked trailers—workers of the parade, security, mechanics for the floats, extras. All of them seemed to be relaxing, settling in for a few hours of quiet now that the parade had started.

"Yeah…" Julie followed his gaze. The tone in her

voice told him that she wasn't picking up what he was putting down.

"They look mostly unoccupied," he went on. "*Unsupervised*. Everyone's attention is on the parade."

Julie studied the parking lot as the implication churned through her head. Finally, she turned and smiled at him. She held out her hand and he took it. "Let's go!"

Hand-in-hand, they ran along the walking path back to the entrance of the parking lot across 79th Street. Nobody paid them any mind as they marched purposefully toward one of the trailers parked among many others.

They stepped inside, and the light from the open doors at the back allowed them to see the many costumes lined along the racks inside.

"Wow," Julie said. "Look at them all." Her fingers traced the sleeves of all the different-colored fabric. She slid her purse off her shoulder and stashed it beside a plastic tote beneath the clothes rack. "I'll have to come back for that later."

"Definitely. For now, let's pick a set and change into them," Brian said. "Quickly, before someone notices."

Julie dove in to the racks, searching for the best costume that they could fit over their clothes. "Nothing that covers our faces. We need to be seen

on TV."

They found some costumes—characters from a kids' TV show—and began to pull them on. Brian kept his eyes trained on anything other than Julie. Sure, they weren't stripping completely, but he still wanted to protect her privacy.

Brian quickly realized that his sweatshirt needed to come off in order for the top of the costume to fit. And when he lifted his shirt, he felt it pull the shirt he had on underneath up along with it, but in the tangle of arms and sleeves above his head, it took him longer than he wanted to fix himself. When he finally did, he saw Julie quickly turn away.

Except, in the curious glance, he suddenly noticed just how close the two of them had become in the trailer. They were practically standing on top of each other. He could smell the shampoo in her hair—something with coconut—and he could only imagine how soft her perfect skin felt beneath his touch. And her lips looked plump and kissable and—

Julie had stopped moving. Her body had turned so that she was facing him. Both of them half dressed in an absurd costume, but neither of them paying any attention to it.

Brian cleared his throat. "This, uh…this trailer is pretty tight—small. This trailer is *small.*"

Julie giggled—she had the most wonderful little laugh. And a very genuine, sweet smile. One that made the pit of his stomach burn, like he wasn't worthy of the attention, but would do anything to have it again.

"Yeah, it is," she said.

His eyes were locked on her lips. "I could go stand outside while you change if you want—"

She grabbed him, pulling him in at the waist, closing the distance until their lips were pressed against one another's. His hands found their way to the back of her head and he pulled her closer—if that was even possible. As the burning in his stomach continued, he felt like he couldn't get enough. Couldn't get close enough.

His fingers worked through her hair—soft and silky, despite the long day of travel. His other hand moved to her back, feeling the soft fabric of the inner lining of her jacket, and the cotton of her T-shirt, and the muscle under her skin.

He pulled away. It was all getting too much. He wanted her—wanted to kiss her more. But he had just broken up with Kendra a little more than twelve hours ago. Were these feelings he had toward Julie genuine, or the product of loneliness? Of sorrow for what had been lost? The hope and the vision for the future that he had once thought were a sure thing with another woman?

"Are you okay?" Her eyes searched his for an answer.

"Yes. And thank you! That was…that was nice." Why were words so hard for him? He had been with Kendra for three years. They had done a lot more than kiss. And yet he felt a little shy. Not quite like himself. Maybe he was just rusty with all of this flirting interaction.

Or maybe it was Julie.

"Well, that's a first." She laughed. "I've never had a guy thank me for a kiss before."

Finding a little bravado, Brian said, "That's because you've never kissed *me* before."

She leaned up on her toes and planted another kiss on his lips that sent a rush of heat through his body. How had a stranger so quickly captivated him like that?

"Play your cards right and it won't be the last time," she said with a smirk.

Brian bit back another smile, although he knew that his face showed just how happy he was. "I didn't think you were interested in me like that."

"To be honest, when I first saw you I thought you were only *semi*-attractive."

"Gee, thanks," he said with a snicker.

"But now I think you're…well, you're okay." Her

smile showed just how much she was holding back.

"Well, I *guess* you're attractive," he admitted.

"There you go guessing again. You need to stop that. Just say that I'm attractive."

"And inflate your ego even more? I don't think so!"

Julie turned serious, then asked, "You really didn't think that I was interested in you like that? We've kind of been flirting all day."

Brian had thought so, but he didn't want to confuse it with wishful thinking, either. Since his breakup with Kendra was so fresh, he didn't want to have any mixed feelings. Never mind what was going on in his head.

She took his hand. "Thank you for helping me with this crazy goal."

"Of course. Even if it was all to impress your friends back home."

She shook her head. "Not anymore. I've realized that the people worth spending my time with are the people who would help a complete stranger do something incredible." She squeezed his hand, indicating that she meant him. Lifting to her toes, she kissed him again.

Brian's eyes closed naturally as Julie's lips met his. A deep, satisfying sigh escaped him as he broke the kiss and pressed his forehead to hers. "I could really like you."

His eyes opened enough to see her bite her bottom lip. "I could really like you, too."

Brian thought about it. He would like it very much if there were more kisses with Julie. But how could there be? He was going to be moving back to New York. She lived Upstate—or, as Julie would put it: *Western* New York. Either way, it was still on the other side of the state.

And then there was the fact that his long-term relationship had just blown up in his face. He hadn't even begun to pick up the pieces from that before Julie came into his life. He hadn't processed anything about what had happened between him and Kendra. It wouldn't be fair to Julie to pursue something with her if he was still unpacking the trauma from the last girl. Better to end things early before either of them got hurt.

He cleared his throat and took a step back, pulling his hand out of hers. "It's too bad that nothing could ever happen between us."

"It couldn't?" Julie's eyebrows scrunched together in confusion—and pain.

"Well, no. You live, what? Six hours away?"

She nodded. "Eight by train. I looked it up last night. That's how I decided on the bus instead."

"Right," he said with a shrug, faking

nonchalance. "See? It's too far. This would never work. Besides, we don't really know each other. We've just met. And we come from opposite worlds. We have different goals in life. We're in different places now."

Julie's face turned down. It was as if a dark cloud had passed over her. Slowly, she nodded. "Yeah. I guess you're right. So after today, we'll probably never see each other again."

The burning in the pit of Brian's stomach turned to an ache. He wanted to see a lot more of Julie. But that was never going to happen. Once they got in the parade, they would go their separate ways and simply be memories to each other.

"Yeah," he said, trying to conceal his disappointment. "Our lives are just too far apart to have any kind of future between us."

He thought that if he said the words enough that they would be true. If he told himself over and over again that nothing about him and Julie together made sense, romantically, then maybe his feelings would change. But the thing about feelings was that they didn't listen to rational thought. They didn't listen at all. They just were.

And Brian was a mess of all different kinds of feelings. None of which he was ready to unpack and sort through just yet.

"But," he added hopefully, "it doesn't mean we can't make the most of the time we have left together."

The hint of a smile returned to her face. It was a sad one. "Yeah. I'd like that."

Silently, they turned away from each other and finished dressing in their costumes.

Chapter Ten
Thanksgiving
Julie

Brian and I power-walked through the park. We had made our way back closer to the parade route, and the crowd along the sidewalk had grown. The enormous balloons shaped like characters towered over the trees. As I tried to keep up with Brian, I couldn't help but stare in awe of them. If I hadn't known any better, the balloons looked like they wouldn't fit between the buildings.

Our costumes had become warm, despite the chillier weather. The bright fall sun was enough to create sweat suits, and the fast pace that we moved at didn't help any.

Truth be told, I was over it. Even though I was still wonderstruck by the parade, I didn't care to become a part of it anymore. I didn't care to achieve some stupid goal set during some stupid night at our stupid hometown bar.

Brian had been right. The whole thing was stupid. I just wanted to go home.

The trouble was, home wasn't a good place to be, either. Not with my mother mad at me and all the expectations of Thanksgiving—and soon, Christmas—mounting. Maybe I even regretted coming to New York City at all.

No. If I hadn't gotten on that bus, I never would've met Brian. And without meeting Brian, I wouldn't have felt…what? This crush on a boy who will never be the perfect fit for me? The thrill each time he took my hand? The ache to press my lips against his again?

And yet…I couldn't deny the pull. I couldn't deny the fact that I wanted to learn everything about him. I couldn't deny the way he made me feel. I couldn't deny just how great his lips felt on mine.

We came to a walkway that led us to the crowded sidewalk. Brian looked over at me with a smile that I couldn't return. Immediately, his faded away.

"Are you okay?" he asked.

I shrugged. I couldn't tell him that I no longer cared to get in the parade. Not with all the time and effort he had put into it. For me.

Brian's shoulders sagged and he turned to me. "I'm sorry for hurting you before. I didn't mean to. I was just trying to protect us before either of us got hurt. I didn't realize—"

"It's okay," I blurted before he could say out loud what we were both thinking: I cared more for him than either of us realized. "There's nothing we can do." I scoffed, my words trailing out of me without thought, all so I could hold him off from adding any of his own. Any sympathies my way. Anything to make me feel like the fool that I was. "Not unless I transferred schools to one in New York—and then there's the higher cost of tuition. Or I could take online classes, but I've already registered for next semester—besides all that, where would I even live if I moved here?" I shook my head. "Never mind. Forget all of that. It's a stupid idea. We just met last night!"

But, oh, what a long night it had been. From the bus ride to the trip to his mother's house to almost getting caught in the park to the kiss in the trailer to now, every moment had felt like a day in and of itself. It was like I had known Brian for a week. And even that wouldn't be enough to base a decision to move across the state on.

We had to think rationally. Just the facts. And the fact was, we didn't really know each other.

Brian nodded and looked down at the leaves brushing against his oversized costumed shoe. "Yeah, you're right. We don't know each other that well."

I took in a deep breath, pushing it out loudly to cover for the fact that it was a little shaky. The prospect of never seeing Brian again was almost more than I could bear to think about.

"Hey, aren't you guys supposed to be in the parade?" someone on the sidewalk asked us.

We both looked up at him, immediately pulled out of our heartbreak, then looked at each other. Suddenly, we were both reminded of the outside world existing around us while it felt like ours was crashing down.

"Yeah, we are," Brian called to him, then turned back to me. "What do you say? If we run, we might be able to catch up to our float." He extended his gloved hand.

I stared at it. His hand felt like a loaded offer. But was I just being dramatic? He was just a boy. I couldn't let him derail my whole life.

But what kind of life had I been living? Going to the neighborhood bar. Spending time with people who didn't genuinely care for me or want to see me succeed. Taking wild and dangerous dares, all for clout in the same small town I was desperate to escape.

If I wanted changes in my life, now was the time to start making them. To start *truly* living my life. I felt more alive in the last twelve hours than I had over the last several years.

I took Brian's hand—clumsy and awkward since we were both in costume. That helped us break the tension as we laughed. Then, I said simply, "Let's go."

His own smile broke out and we ran down the sidewalk, navigating among the crowd, tethered together by our obnoxious costumes that made the crowd part as we came through. I'm sure we looked like complete fools with our costumes, but I didn't care. I didn't know any of these people. And clearly, neither did Brian.

We lucked out that the costumes we picked went with a float that had a large balloon rising up from it, so it was easy to spot as we ran. We also lucked out that parades moved relatively slow, this one being no exception since it was a major community- and nation-wide event.

Within five minutes we had worked our way down the sidewalk so that we were a little ways ahead of the float. That would give us some time to get out in the parade in time for the float to come by.

If all went according to plan.

More shouts and outrage came from around us as we worked our way to the barricades, but with the large costumes the complaints were hard to hear. And many of them died off once they saw us. They probably figured we were workers trying to get in the parade and not just jerks trying to get to the front of the line.

Exactly what we wanted.

There was a guard standing at the barricade whose eyes locked on us as we got closer to the barricade. We were kind of hard to miss in our costumes.

Once we were in front of him, Brian breathlessly spat out a story. "Overslept! Got to the trailer! Costumes! Parade left without us!"

The guard raised his eyebrows and leaned in slightly. "You overslept?"

Both of us nodded. Seemed like as good an excuse as any.

"But you're supposed to be on the float?"

More nods.

The guard sighed, then looked up and down at the parade. He spotted the one with the corresponding balloon, then extended his arm. "That one?"

Again, we nodded. It was bad enough we told one lie, so for the rest of the story we were going to have to rely on assumptions on the guard's part. Anything to preserve our conscience.

He looked around for another guard. Not finding one, he turned back to us and began to part the barricade. "Okay. But make it quick. And don't be late next year!"

Next year. If only.

The guard allowed us to pass while holding off the crowd with his arm.

We tossed a "thank you!" over our shoulders as we darted to the float, which was now right in front of us. Finding the ladder in the back of the float, we climbed on.

And that's when it hit me: I made it. I was in the Thanksgiving Day Parade.

I raised my phone and snapped a selfie with the giant balloon in the background. Then I took a video of the float, the crowd lining the sidewalk, the marchers beside the float who were waving at the crowd as we moved along the parade route.

Someone else on the float glared at me through her costume. "What are you *doing*? Phones are *strictly* against the rules!"

Immediately I put my phone down. I could send the pictures to my social media later. I was too intoxicated with the rush of being in the parade to care about the possibility that I might be removed from it. Still, I didn't want to get anyone else on the float in trouble so I slipped my phone back inside my

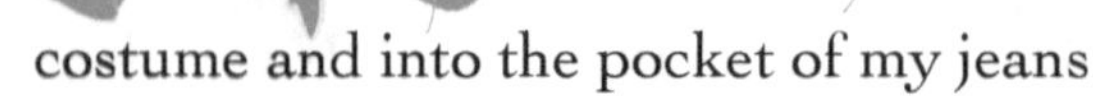

costume and into the pocket of my jeans.

"Careful," Brian warned. "Don't want to get us kicked off when we just got on." He turned and waved to the crowd, enjoying the moment just as much as me.

"Sorry. I just wanted to get some proof for Eric."

He turned to me, his wave losing its enthusiasm as his arm lowered slowly to his side. "Eric? Who's that?"

"Oh, this guy back home." I waved, thinking about how great it would feel to have Eric see me here and know that I was a woman of my word. Not that I cared about impressing him anymore. At this point, it was more to show him that I followed through with plans.

That I was accountable.

Reliable.

Everything he wasn't.

Eric only cared about himself and having a good time, even if it was at the expense of someone else.

I scoffed. "Actually, I had a crush on him. That's why I agreed to the dare. I thought it would give him a reason to like me, too."

Saying it out loud was freeing. I had finally addressed the feelings that had been building for a while. Casted them away as a silly crush. That's all that it was. There was no future for me and Eric. And now that I had said it out loud, I could finally move on.

"Oh," Brian said beside me. "Yeah. Well, when we get up to the TV cameras, I hope that Kendra is watching back home."

Kendra.

The noise and excitement of the parade faded around me, dulling my senses as if I were falling into a black hole. The name struck me and reminded me of my reality: I didn't belong here. And after the parade ended, I would have to go back home, where I also didn't feel like I belonged. Brian's family had mentioned Kendra. Had expected to see her come home for Thanksgiving with him, but instead I was there.

"Hey, Brian…" I started.

"Yeah?" he asked as he waved to the crowd on the other side.

"Who's Kendra?"

"Oh, she's my girlfriend."

His words struck me to my core. His *girlfriend*? Since when did he have a girlfriend?

But that would explain why his family had been expecting this Kendra girl instead of me. And why Brian had originally been so distant from me on the bus.

No, but he kissed me. Or rather…*I* kissed *him*.

Both times. But he hadn't stopped it. In fact, he had been the one to tell me that he liked me.

Actually, what he had said was that he *could* like me. Maybe the distance excuse was just that…an excuse. Maybe the only thing holding him back from pursuing anything with me was that he had a girlfriend. Maybe he didn't care about me like he said he did.

Were there any stand-up guys that I was attracted to?

My body slumped and I turned away. Brian remained oblivious — or maybe it was that he chose to ignore me. Either way, I was getting off of this float. I was getting out of this parade. I was done allowing people — allowing *men* — to make a fool of me.

The float was coming around a corner. I used the distraction, and the change in the marching pattern, to my advantage and slipped down the small ladder at the back of the float to disappear into the crowd.

Chapter Eleven
Thanksgiving
Brian

Brian waved to the crowd, smiling at the many faces. All kinds of people were drawn to the spectacle of the parade. Young and old, black or white, families or friends. Everyone seemed to be enjoying the parade.

He focused so much on the crowd because he was trying not to pay any attention to Julie. He was mad at her. How could she still want to impress that loser back home? The one who pushed her to go to a strange city that she'd never been to before, all so he could get a good laugh when she came back and told him about it?

Brian didn't know much about this Eric guy, but what could she see in him? From the little Julie had said about him, even Brian could tell that he was a terrible person who didn't deserve someone like Julie.

That kiss still lingered on Brian's lips. And the fact that their time together was almost over was hard to face, especially when coupled with the fact that there was no future together between them. How could there be?

But if their time together was coming to an end, Brian didn't want to spend it fighting. He didn't want to spoil the time they had had so far. He needed to force his feelings down and treat Julie the same way he always had. If he could.

He turned back toward her to say something—anything—in order to get the conversation going again, but when he looked where she had been standing, she was gone.

His eyes scanned the back of the float, head swiveling back and forth in a panic looking for her. What if something had happened to her? What if security caught wind of them not officially being part of the parade and carted her off? What if something worse had happened?

Finally, he saw her, on the street, jogging to the barricades that lined the parade route. There, a security guard stopped her. He was a thin black man, who wore the standard security guard uniform, but with a sense of authority that had been missing from some of the other guards. He held his place and gestured back to the float, but Julie refused to move.

Brian jumped off the back of the float and nearly collided with one of the walkers, who glared at him before plastering on a smile and waving to the crowd. He ignored them and hurried over to Julie.

"Please, just let me out!" Julie said to the guard.

"You have a job to do! Get back up on that float!" the guard said. "Before you cause an even bigger scene!"

"I'm not even supposed to be here! I'm not part of the parade! I'm a stowaway!"

"Julie!" Brian called when he caught up to her. She refused to meet his eyes, and he felt the sting in his chest. The cold shoulder didn't feel so good. Instead, he refocused his attention on the guard. "What's the problem here?"

"The problem is, you two are supposed to be working! Just like I am!"

"Come on, *please*, just let me go!" Julie put her dramatically oversized costumed hands together. "You're causing the bigger scene by arguing!"

The guard stood taller, hiking up his pants by his belt. His eyes were serious, daring Julie to accuse him even more of not doing his job well.

Brian grabbed Julie's arm and led her down the barricade.

"Hey!" the guard called. "Where are you going! Get back to work!"

Brian ignored him and kept walking along the barricades until he found a spot where two of the pieces weren't hooked together properly and they broke through into the crowd.

"Hey!" the guard called after them again, but didn't move from his post on the other side of the barricades. "You stop right there if you know what's good for you!"

Brian pushed through the crowd until they came out on the other side, where the number of people were fewer. He looked around for street signs to get his bearings: 6th Avenue and 56th Street. He led Julie down the street, ignoring the other distractions of the city, until they found a spot that was secluded enough for the two of them to talk.

At least, that's what Brian had hoped for. But when they got away from the crowd, Julie wrenched her arm away from his and stalked off further down the street, wiping at her face.

"Are you crying?" he asked softly as he came up behind her. He put his hand on her shoulder, but she shrugged him off. "What's the matter? Are you mad at me?"

What a stupid question. Of course she was. He knew that. He just wasn't sure exactly why, or if she would ever be able to forgive him for whatever he did in the short amount of time that they had left.

"Just forget it," she said, still not looking at him. "It's stupid."

Brian stood and let her cry for a moment. He looked up and down the street. On one end, the parade was moving by with the giant balloons seemingly squeezing between the skyscrapers, on the other end of the street, cars moved past the intersection as if it were a regular day.

"I have to be honest, Julie, I don't really understand—and I want to," he said. "We were just on the parade—something you said you wanted. I thought you'd be happy."

She sniffled and shook her head, finally picking it up, even though her back was still to him. "It doesn't matter."

"Oh, sure, right," he said, his anger seeping into his voice despite his efforts to keep it at bay. "I just spent all morning running around the city with you, but after all that, you spent *two seconds* on the float and then walk off without a word and tell me that it doesn't matter?"

She turned to him and wiped the tears away from her red and swollen eyes. "I know. I'm sorry. Thanks for helping me get on the float. You're a man of your word." Another swipe of her tears and she began to pull off the ridiculous costume. "But I think I'll find my way back to the bus station on my own now." She stumbled as she pulled off the costume, dropping it to the sidewalk. Then, without waiting for an answer, she turned and started off down the street.

"Julie, wait!" He scrambled to pick up the costume before realizing that Julie mattered more. He dropped it back down and jogged to catch up with her. "Do you even have any idea where the bus stop *is*?"

"I'll figure it out." She tossed a wave over her shoulder as she walked, refusing to stop to look at him.

He was power-walking now—Julie had quite the stride—but he fell into step with her. "I'm not just going to leave you on the street."

Julie stopped abruptly and turned on him. She looked him up and down. "Please. I made it to New York without your help, I think I can make it *out* of here by myself, too." She turned and began to stalk off down the sidewalk again.

Brian rushed to catch up to her, this time running in front of her and putting his hands on her shoulders to stop her in her tracks.

"Get out of my way," she said. "You helped me, I thanked you, it was fun, and now it's over. Why won't you leave me alone?"

"Because I like you! I don't want to see you upset. Even if you are still hung up on someone else."

Julie's eyes searched his. He could tell that she had a lot of thoughts swirling around her head, on the verge of escaping, but none of it was shared. She cleared her throat. "Well, ignore me. Forget I existed. There's no future between us, just like you said."

"Is that why you're upset?" he asked. "The distance thing?"

"No, it's not the *distance thing*," she blurted. "I just have no interest in dating someone who is dating someone else."

"Ah," he said. "So that's what it is. Kendra."

"Yeah. *Kendra*. You know, *your girlfriend*?"

"She's not my girlfriend—not anymore."

Julie reared back, her brows scrunching. "She's not?"

"No, we broke up."

She studied him, not convinced that she was hearing the truth. "Then why did you say that she was?"

"Because I wanted to hurt you!" he said. "The truth is…Kendra cheated on me. I walked in on her in bed with someone else. In *our* bed. The one that we shared together. That we…" His words trailed off and he looked away. He swallowed, then added,

"That's why I really came back home. It wasn't just for Thanksgiving."

She seemed to sober at the revelation. "Oh. So she's an ex?"

"Yeah. It's over between us."

Julie was quiet, then her eyes narrowed. "Wait a minute…your family expected to see *her* this morning and not me. Which means they didn't know that the two of you had broken up. When did this breakup happen?"

Brian diverted his eyes again. "Um…yesterday."

She nodded slowly. "Ah. Right. Okay, so I'm still leaving."

"What?" he asked. "Why? I just told you the truth! I said it was over!"

"Yeah, and as much as I have no interest in dating someone who is dating someone else, I *also* have no interest in being somebody's rebound girl." She tossed the words over her shoulder as she started down the street again.

"You're not a—"

She turned on him, pointing a finger at him. "Yes! That's exactly what I'd be! A rebound! Isn't that why you kissed me earlier? To get over whatever you were feeling for Kendra? Because you were sad that you lost her? Because you were lonely?"

"No, I kissed you because I like you!" he argued.

"And let's not forget that *you* kissed *me* first!"

Julie pulled back, but didn't walk away. Her eyes drifted to the noise of the parade, happy and excited as it passed by not even a full block away.

"I wasn't expecting to like you, Julie," he said after a few quiet moments. "But I do. A lot."

She hugged herself and shrugged. "Well, that's too bad." There was a crack in her voice. "Because I'm tired of being the fool. The stupid girl who destroyed her holiday over some stupid boy—two stupid boys, actually."

"Me and Eric?"

She nodded. "I'm done with him. And I'm done with you. I just want to go home—and if you knew what kind of home I'm going back to, you'd know that's no comfort." She studied him. "Goodbye, Brian."

He considered her. She clearly was not in the mood to talk. And he didn't want to beg and plead with her to do it. So he had to let her go. This was it.

"There's nothing I can do to stop you? To change your mind?" he asked.

"And do what?" Julie asked. "I don't live here, Brian. I don't belong. We don't know each other. This thing between us is just a stupid crush. We got caught up in the moment. There's nothing here."

Even though he knew her words were true on the

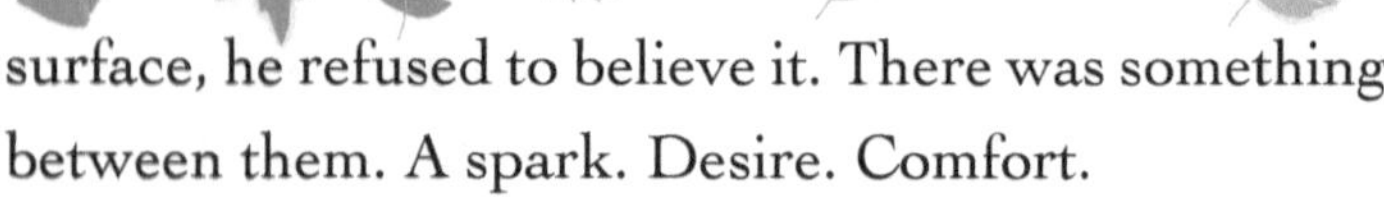

surface, he refused to believe it. There was something between them. A spark. Desire. Comfort.

But was all of that enough to make such monumental changes? Brian knew he was already moving back to New York, but Julie would have to make a complete lifestyle change. And what if she was right and they didn't work out? She would be making all the sacrifices for him, just like he'd done for Kendra.

No. He wasn't going to force her to do something she didn't want to do. No matter how hard it was for him to accept.

"Goodbye, Julie." His voice cracked a bit. "I had fun. Until…"

"Yeah," she said. "Me too. And thanks again." Turning, she started down the sidewalk. This time, without him trying to stop her.

The sound of a marching band in the parade hit his ears now that the conversation was over. It was like coming back to reality. He wondered if they had just started or if they'd been playing all along. It was so hard to focus on other things when he felt so empty, now that another woman—the second in twenty-four hours—had left him.

This was, hands-down, the worst Thanksgiving ever.

Chapter Twelve
Thanksgiving
Brian

Brian's body was cold and tired. He had spent most of the afternoon walking around, trying to clear his head. He had made it back to the park, where he returned his and Julie's costumes to the trailer. What a sight he must've been as he carried both costumes over his shoulder as he navigated the long route around the parade.

Back at the parking lot with the trailers, Brian had found where they had stashed Julie's bag. He carried it around for longer than any man typically would want to carry around a purse. Between the purse and the costumes, he actually preferred the purse—not that he'd ever admit that out loud. It was just easier to carry. And,

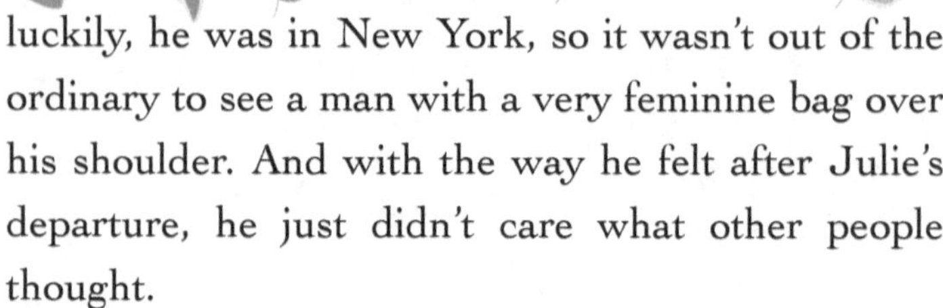

luckily, he was in New York, so it wasn't out of the ordinary to see a man with a very feminine bag over his shoulder. And with the way he felt after Julie's departure, he just didn't care what other people thought.

Back at his mother's apartment, he walked through the door and saw his whole family sitting at the table, dressed in their holiday best, with the Thanksgiving feast spread out on the table. The kids were running wild, having grown impatient from waiting. And when Jeffrey saw Brian walk through the door, he tossed his cloth napkin on the table and grumbled.

"*There* he is! It's about time you showed up!"

His wife smacked his arm and gave him a sour look.

Again, Brian didn't really care.

"What's with the purse, dude?" Mark asked.

Their mother hushed him as she rose from the table to greet her youngest son. "You have perfect timing. We were just sitting down to eat."

"We've been sitting for almost an hour now..." Jeffrey grumbled.

Their mother shot him a look while the wives both smacked him.

"Sorry," Brian murmured.

"Honey, what's the matter?" his mother asked.

"Yeah, where's Julie?" Mark asked. "Mom made room for her."

Brian shook his head. Before, when he had just broken up with Kendra, he had thought this dinner was going to be hard. Now, he knew it would be impossible. "She went back home."

Rebecca got up and gave him a quick hug, then stood by him and rubbed his back. "I'm sorry to hear that."

"Me too."

"Yeah, she seemed nice," Tina added.

He nodded, his eyes trained on the floor, unable to look any of his family in the face. "She was." Then, quieter, "I miss her."

Silence fell over the room, other than the sound of children's television. The kids had finally settled on the couches, absorbed by the animations.

Brian's mother rubbed his back and ushered him out of the room. "Brian, why don't you help me bring out the rest of the dishes from the kitchen?"

"Ma, you already brought—" Mark started, but Rebecca slapped him on the back of the head as she retook her seat.

Even though he knew it was a distraction, Brian welcomed the escape and followed his mother out of the room. There, in the relative privacy, she pulled a dish towel that had been hanging on the oven and

smacked him across the chest with it.

"Are you crazy?" she hissed.

He rubbed at his chest where the towel had hit him. "Ow. What was that for?"

"To wake you up," she said. "You need to stop acting like a damn fool and stop moping around."

"A fool? Mom, it's been a long week."

She sighed and crossed her arms. "Okay. I'm sorry, honey. What's been going on? Where's Kendra?"

"We…we broke up." He shook his head. He didn't want to tell her too much more. His mother had loved Kendra—all of his family did. To destroy that image of who she was—their good, happy memories of her—would just be cruel.

Most of all, though, he didn't want the looks of sympathy his family would inevitably give him if they knew the truth about why they had broken up. He didn't want them to diminish the new feelings he had for Julie if they knew what Kendra had done. At least, not until Brian had had time to reconcile those thoughts and feelings himself.

"Well, I gathered that much," his mother said. "Why else would you ditch her for Thanksgiving— even if it wasn't *her* Thanksgiving?" She softened her stance and cupped his cheek. "You want to tell me what happened, sweetie?"

"Not really."

"Are you okay?"

He shrugged. "About Kendra? Yeah, I'm getting there." In truth, he had seen the end coming for a while, although he didn't expect things to have blown up *quite* the way that they had. He had thought that Kendra would at least have the courtesy to break up with him *before* she jumped in bed with someone else.

Then again, her infidelity gave him the out he never knew he was looking for. The one that led him to Julie. And he wouldn't trade that for anything— no matter how it ended.

"Okay, so now tell me what happened with this other girl—Julie." She leaned back against the counter and muttered with a smirk, "You certainly get around."

Brian shot her a look. "It's not like that."

"Well, you can't deny how it seems, my love."

"I know, but...I don't know. Julie is just—well, Julie lives on the other side of the state."

"So?" his mother asked with a shoulder shrug.

"It'll never work."

"Says who?"

"Says me. And her. Neither one of us are interested in the long-distance thing," he said. "Especially when I need to deal with untangling myself from Kendra's life in Canada. I still have a bunch of stuff at her apartment, and then there's the visa, and work, and—"

She waved her hand. "Oh, honey, we can help with that. We're family! We take care of each other. That's what we do. But Julie…" She shook her head. "Honey, if you like this girl, then you need to stop being an idiot."

"Mom—"

She raised a finger. "Just stop talking and listen to your mother, for once. I can tell that you like her—"

"You only met her once!"

She waved her finger. "You interrupt me again and I'll get the ladle—don't think I won't! You might be taller than me now, but I'm still your mother!"

Brian smiled, remembering when she used to threaten that when they were kids. "Okay. Go on."

"I'm not sure what happened between you and Kendra, but I can tell you one thing: I knew you two weren't a good fit."

His eyes widened. "But you loved her."

"Of course I did! She was funny as hell. But honey, she was not the one for you." She tapped her chest. "A mother knows these things."

"Why didn't you say anything?"

"And dictate your life like that? No, honey, I didn't want to meddle. And besides, I'm your mother,

I'm not *you*. If you said you loved her, then I needed to trust your instincts. I knew I'd always be around to help you pick up the pieces just in case you were wrong. And now here we are."

Yes, they were indeed. He wondered if it would've been better if his mother had told him her thoughts on his relationship with Kendra. But then, if she had, he probably would've written off her concerns and looked for excuses to explain away Kendra's behavior—including the affair. Even though it hurt, it was probably better that it worked out the way that it had.

"But Julie is a different story," she went on. "It's obvious she's a much better fit for you."

He scoffed and rolled his eyes. "Please, Mom. You never really talked to her."

"Well, no, but after the two of you left this morning, the girls and I looked her up online. Did you know she's famous on social media?"

Brian thought calling Julie "famous" was a stretch, but he figured she probably had a decent number of followers based on the amount of pictures and videos she had taken.

"Yeah," he said simply. "She mentioned it."

"Anyway, we saw all her posts," his mom went on. "Of course, she has selfies and that, but she has a lot of candid pictures with her friends. Pictures of different trips she's been on — oh, and *a lot* of pictures from the library while she studies."

"Mom, you can't get a full picture of someone based on what they put online." The underlying message: social media is a mask that everyone uses to put their best foot forward. It's not reality.

"Well, no. I know that. But you know what can't be edited and filtered?" she asked.

He humored her. "What's that?"

"Your smile every time you looked at her. The way your eyes lit up when she was taking another picture. Your banter back and forth."

That surprised him. Had Julie captured that much of their morning together? She had been on her phone *a lot*, but he didn't realize she had been pointing her phone at him. Now he was curious to look her up himself. But that would mean bringing up all kinds of memories — especially the ones from how they had left things.

"We all decided that she was perfect for you," his mother went on. "Even your brothers looked at her profile and agreed that she was, as they put it, 'a catch.'" She laughed. "You *both* looked so happy together."

Brian considered her words. Everything with Julie had come so naturally. He never felt like he needed to put on an act, and never felt that Julie was doing the same. Neither of them expected any kind of long-term social tie to form out of their chance meeting, so the masks and personas fell by the wayside, leaving just them to be themselves.

Julie *was* beautiful.

He *did* enjoy spending time with her.

He *did* feel happier with her.

And that *kiss* was what he'd remember most of all.

"No, Mom," he said with a shake of his head. "No. It's too late. She's already on her way home."

"Did she drive?"

"No, she took the bus. That's how we met. On the way into the city."

His mother smiled. "On the same bus as you?"

He nodded.

"Then it's perfect!"

"*How* is any of this perfect? This is all the opposite of perfect, Mom."

She put her hands on his shoulders. "Honey, we checked the bus schedule! The next bus out of New York isn't until eight o'clock tonight! That means that Julie's still in the city, and has nowhere to go."

"So what am I supposed to do? Bring her back here? Give her turkey and pie, then wish her well on her trip back home?"

She rolled her eyes again. "Oh, I just want to

shake you." And she did, in fact, shake him. "What you do is you go talk to her. Tell her how you feel — and *be honest*. If it's meant to be, you two will make it work. And if it's not, then you'll be able to get over it."

"But she lives—"

"Listen honey, distance is irrelevant in this day and age. Hell, you moved to a whole other *country* for a year and we still kept in touch!" She softened and said, "If you really like her—and I know that you do—then take a chance and go get her. Otherwise, you'll regret it for the rest of your life."

She stepped back from him and raised her hands in a surrender gesture. "Now, I've said my piece. I'll leave you here to think it over. I know you'll make the right decision. *That's* the way I raised you."

And with that, she was gone, into the next room to rejoin the rest of the family at the dinner table.

While Brian stood in the kitchen and debated his choices, he heard his mother call for the family to start eating because, "This bird is getting cold!"

Brian thought about what his mother had said. The first thought he had was that she was annoying. The second was that she was right. And the third was that he wasn't ready to lose Julie, no matter how long their relationship had lasted—if they could even call it that. Either way, he wanted to see her again.

So without saying goodbye to his family, and even though his feet were killing him from his long afternoon walk, he stepped out of the kitchen, grabbed Julie's purse from where he had dropped it on the floor, and stepped out of the apartment.

He didn't know if he and Julie had a future, but there was one thing he did know: he wasn't going to let Julie sit out on the cold sidewalk on Thanksgiving.

Chapter Thirteen
Thanksgiving
Julie

I managed to make it back to the bus stop, with the help of Google Maps, which, thanks to the crowd from the parade, took forever to load and sucked even more of my phone battery that had already been diminishing. I did bring my charger with me, but I had left it in my purse, which, for all I knew, was sitting in the costume trailer back at the park. If it hadn't been moved already. My wallet, containing my license and credit cards, were in there, just as Brian had warned. But at the time I didn't really care. I just wanted to get out of New York City.

I paced up and down the sidewalk on 34th Street, where the bus had dropped me off earlier that morning.

It was quiet, although not completely devoid of people. There were a few people jogging on the High Line, which started just down the street a little. Another man stood on the corner a ways up, seemingly waiting for something or someone, but it was impossible to tell exactly what he was doing. Of course, not being accustomed to these urban settings, I assumed he was selling drugs, but it was probably something innocent.

At least, I hoped.

After another lap up and down the sidewalk, I checked my phone again. The battery was at ten percent and the time was only two minutes later than the last time I'd checked.

I brought up the website for bus tickets, not surprised to find that nothing had changed from when I checked a couple hours ago. The next bus still wasn't until eight o'clock at night. I debated whether to purchase a ticket but two things held me back. The first was that there was a feeling of unfinished business still in New York. I wanted to get out but somehow I couldn't quite bring myself to go through the motions to make that happen.

The other was that I didn't have my credit card information with me to make the purchase. Even if I did, my phone was about to die. How would I show the QR code to the driver when I boarded?

It was just my luck.

"Damn, I'm an idiot," I muttered to myself as I closed out of the web browser on my phone. The battery had drained to seven percent. I hadn't thought any of this through. The sudden midnight trip to New York. Navigating the city. Most importantly, getting home. I had been lucky so far, but now my luck had run out.

My stomach ached with hunger. I hadn't had anything to eat all day, and since I had lost my purse, I had no means to buy any food. Not unless I found a place that was open on Thanksgiving that would take pity on me.

But hey, I did it. I made it in the parade. I had pictures and videos to prove it. For what? All for Eric to be surprised and Brittany and the other guys to talk about it for all of five minutes before moving on to their next stupid idea?

Why did I let other people control my actions so easily? Never again.

I hugged myself, feeling the November chill settle in as the day made way for evening. That was another thing I had forgotten, just how cold it would be down here near the water. Maybe I'd be better off finding a Starbucks or something to hang out in until morning—were they even open all night? Would they be open on a holiday? I had no idea.

Add that to the list of things I had failed to think about before I came to the city.

I wished that Brian were still with me. Even Eric. Hell, at this point, I even missed my mother. I just wanted company. Someone to help figure things out for me. As if this situation I found myself in wasn't completely my own fault.

My phone buzzed with a text. Desperate for interaction, I nearly dropped it as I quickly raised it to look at the screen.

It was from Brittany, sent to our group chat with Eric, Chloe, Tony, and Otto.

> JULES! CHLOE SAID YOU MADE IT TO NYC! DIDN'T SEE YOU ON TV. PARADE? PICS OR IT DIDN'T HAPPEN!

Out of habit, I started typing out a reply and attached some pictures. But then I saw the other names in the text.

Eric.

Tony.

Otto.

Brittany.

Chloe.

Other than Chloe, none of the rest of them cared about the fact that I sacrificed my days off to be the butt of their joke. To somehow prove myself to them, as if my friendship were conditional.

The other comments began to come through in my silence.

Tony

BET SHE DIDN'T EVEN GO.

Otto

SHE WENT, BUT SHE PROBABLY DIDN'T EVEN SEE THE PARADE.

Eric

JULIE, YOU POSTED SO MANY PICTURES! WERE YOU ACTUALLY ON THE PARADE, OR ARE YOU JUST REALLY GOOD AT FOOLING EVERYONE? ;)

That's when I remembered how liberally I had been posting pictures and stories online all day. And even with all of that proof, all of that evidence so blatantly shoved in their faces, my so-called friends *still* didn't believe me.

And then another thought occurred to me. It was just after four. I knew my family usually had Thanksgiving dinner around this time every year. Why were Brittany, Eric, and the guys so worried about what I was doing hundreds of miles away when they should've been spending this time with their families? Hell, I didn't even *like* my family and I would've had my focus on them during Thanksgiving dinner.

These weren't my people, and I knew that now. The people I had called my friends all these years were shallow, and I no longer wanted to swim in the shallow end.

My thumb tapped the backspace button again and again until my drafted text and all of my pictures were deleted. They didn't deserve a response. They didn't deserve the recognition of making me the butt of their joke. I wasn't going to be laughed at for even a second. I was done.

My phone buzzed again. This time with an incoming call from Chloe. She had been the exception this whole time, calling me, asking me not to go to New York, offering to pay for me to come home. With all that in mind, I swiped the screen and answered the call.

"Hello?"

"Jules! Are you okay?"

"Yeah." That was a lie.

"Are you on your way home?"

"No."

Chloe sighed on the other end. "You're mad at

me. Jules, I'm sorry for not checking in sooner! I wanted to, but I've been with my family all day and I didn't want to be on my phone when my grandma was asking me about my classes. It's just that I don't see my grandma very much, but now we're just waiting on dessert to be served and I needed to check in with you because—"

"Chloe," I interrupted, "I'm not mad at you. Actually, I'm glad you called. I had a really good morning. And I made it into the parade! I wasn't in it for very long, but—"

"Julie, no offense, but I don't care about the parade," Chloe said. "Not right now, at least. I want to know how you're doing. Where are you? Are you safe?"

I smiled. Chloe wanted to talk to *me*, not just hear my wild story. Most importantly, she wanted to make sure I was okay. *Really* okay. And, it struck me that she had been the first one in the last two days to have done that at all.

"Uh…I'm okay."

"Where are you?" she insisted.

"Standing on the street, waiting for the bus." That wasn't a *total* lie. The bus was coming, even if I didn't have a ticket yet. I considered asking Chloe to pay for one for me. I'd pay her back. But the problem persisted: how would I show the code to the driver when my phone died? Besides, there was that nagging feeling that I wasn't *truly* ready to leave yet.

"By yourself?"

I debated whether I should tell her about Brian, but what was there to tell? He was just a boy who had helped me. And so what if there was a kiss? So what if there were some feelings shared? Brian said it himself: nothing could happen between us. Our lives were too far apart.

Instead, I played it off. "Of course I'm by myself. Who else would I be with?"

"I don't know. You said you're waiting for the bus? When is that coming?"

The truth always does find a way to come out, doesn't it? "Um…tonight."

"What time?"

"It says eight o'clock."

"And you have the ticket ready and everything?"

"Well…" I drew out the word. "I haven't actually bought the ticket yet."

"Why not!" she blurted.

"Um…I kind of lost my purse. With my wallet and everything in it."

She was quiet on the other end. I wondered if she was judging me and my poor choices.

Of course she was.

Everyone was.

That's why Eric, Brittany, and the rest of the them all found it so funny that I had actually come to New York City. Who would be stupid enough to do that?

I was.

And that was funny to them.

Instead, though, Chloe said, "How did you—never mind. You're okay, though?"

"Yeah."

She let out a deep breath. "Okay. Look, Julie, I've been with my family all day, so if you want, I can skip dessert and drive out there to get you. It'll take me a while, and I don't know exactly where I'm going, but I'll manage. I just can't stand the thought of you stranded in the city all by yourself—especially on a holiday."

I could've cried. I *almost* cried. This was one of the most selfless offers anyone had ever done for me. But I couldn't let her do it. Not when I was in this mess as a direct result of my actions.

"No, I can't let you do that," I said to her. "I appreciate the offer. Trust me, I do. More than you could ever know. I love that you want to help me, but I'll be okay. I'll figure it out."

"Julie, this isn't the time to be brave," Chloe said. "The things that go on in that city at night…"

"I know. But I'll just find somewhere warm to stay. Figure out my backup plan. And just wait it out for the bus. Maybe I can convince him to give me a ride back home and pay later. Or something. Let this be a lesson to myself that I shouldn't do stupid things like this again."

Chloe laughed humorlessly. An admission that she agreed that this was a stupid idea.

She didn't even know the half of it.

"Then let me pay for your bus ticket," Chloe offered.

That nagging feeling that I still had unfinished business reared its ugly head again. "No, you don't need to do that." We were in college. Most of us didn't have jobs. And those of us who did needed the money to pay for gas, and books for school. Chloe was as strapped for cash as I was.

The promise of endless drinks at the hometown bar and monthly meals with Eric had long lost its luster.

"I really don't like the idea of you sitting in New York City all by yourself overnight," Chloe said again.

"Neither do I."

"Then let me come and get you."

"And get you lost and stranded, too? No, Chloe. Stay home. Stay with your family. That's where you belong. Besides, I have a backup plan." If worse came to worst, I would have to suck it up and go back to Brian's mother's apartment. Even though I wasn't anything to him, or any of them, and even though they were a full house already, I knew that they'd let me stay there if I needed to. They were good people. All of them. Including Brian.

"I thought you said you needed to figure out your backup plan?"

"Well, it's more complicated than that."

A pause, then, "What aren't you telling me?"

I sighed. Time to come clean about Brian. "Okay, but you can't repeat this to Brittany or the guys."

"Why in the world would I say anything to them?" Chloe asked. "They're jerks."

"I'm serious."

"So am I."

I took another deep breath. "I…met a guy."

The silence indicated Chloe's surprise.

"His name is Brian," I added.

"Okay…" she started slowly. "And how did you meet him?"

"On the bus on the way to New York City. He was really sweet and he actually helped me get in the parade." I smirked at the memory. Brian and I had had a lot of fun.

Had being the key word.

"So you met a guy last night, spent the day with him, and now you think you can stay at his house?" Chloe asked. "Not to sound like the skeptic here, Jules, but I've seen *Dateline* episodes that have started this way. You think you can trust a guy and then—*boom!*—just like that, he's secretly a serial killer."

I smiled now, for a different reason. Chloe and I were talking like normal. Like friends. The fact that I was stranded on the street in New York City was momentarily forgotten. "I can trust him. I know that."

"That's what they say on *Dateline,* too."

"No, I mean, I've met his family. It *is* Thanksgiving after all."

She sighed. "Okay. Go on."

"Anyway, we had a great time this morning. I, uh, I even kissed him in the back of a costume trailer."

"Jules!" Chloe said, as if this were a big scandal. "That's so unlike you! You've been flirting with Eric for a year now and haven't even come close to that."

"I know."

"So does this mean that you're over Eric?"

"Oh yeah," I said. "Definitely. This whole ordeal has shown me just how…*stuck* he is, you know? Like, I'm sure if I jumped in time to a Friday night five years from now, I would still be able to find him in the bar, ordering the same drink he's always been getting, and doing the same impractical jokes he's been doing all along."

"Like sending you to New York City on Thanksgiving?"

I sighed, feeling dumb for having fallen for it. "Yeah."

"I know what you mean," Chloe said. "I've seen it, too. Honestly, the only reason I went out last night was to see you."

I smiled. "Thanks for that, Chloe. I'm glad you called."

"Me too. And I'm glad you're okay, but you're not out of the woods yet. Are you saying that you might go to this Brian's house? I have to be honest, whether you met his family or not, it still makes me nervous."

"More or less nervous than me sleeping on the street?"

Another sigh as she relented to my dilemma. "Is it his apartment or his parents' apartment?"

"His mom's."

"Then I suppose that's your best option. Statistically speaking, women are far less likely to be serial killers than men."

I rolled my eyes at the math major. Chloe was on track to become a high school math teacher, but I wouldn't be surprised if she ended up teaching at the collegiate level someday. Or even working for NASA or something.

"Yeah, I guess it is…"

"You don't sound convinced," she said, picking up on my tone.

"It's just that…Brian and I got into this huge fight," I said. "Hence, why I'm sitting on the street and not stuffing my face with his mother's turkey right about now."

"Doesn't sound like it's her turkey you're after."

"Chloe!" My voice echoed down the street. The man on the corner had moved away and my head swiveled, wondering if he had moved to take advantage of my distraction with the phone conversation or if he had innocently stepped away for something else.

"Sorry. What was the fight about?"

"His girlfriend—or his ex. But they just broke up last night."

"Ooooh."

"Yeah. I told him I didn't want to be a rebound girl, and he said I wasn't, but he broke up with her *last night* and he lived with her—even moved to Canada for her." I shook my head. "There's just too much history there for him to be over her so quickly."

"I'm sorry, Jules. But…given the circumstances, I think you might need to ask him for this favor regardless."

"I don't know if I can go back there."

"You're going to have to. Who knows? Maybe the two of you can talk it out—maybe figure out a way to make it work. Sounds like the two of you have a spark, regardless of what happened last night with him and some other girl."

"What happened to your concerns that I'd end up the subject of another *Dateline* special?"

"Let's not rule that out. All I'm saying is, if this guy helped you step out of your comfort zone and make some other realizations about your life, then he's probably pretty special. Tonight might just be the first step into making some positive changes in your life. You just have to be willing to take that chance."

I focused my attention on the sidewalk. It was stained with something—probably old gum and dirt from the bottom of people's shoes. Over the water across the Hudson River the sun was setting behind the tall buildings in New Jersey.

"Chloe, it's not that simple."

"Sure it is. You said you had a great time with him, right?"

"Yeah."

"And you've met his family?"

"Yeah."

"And they all seem sane?"

"They're all very nice."

"And he's close with them?"

"Seems like it."

"And you met him on the bus?"

I breathed out a frustrated sigh. "I said that."

"And then he spent all day with you, taking you to meet his mother, taking you to the parade, and fulfilling some stupid small town bar dare?"

"What's your point?"

"Jules, it sounds like he has stronger feelings for you than just some rebound fling."

I wasn't convinced. "Or maybe he's just using me to replace what he had with his girlfriend."

"So tell me more about this girlfriend."

"He didn't say much about her." My eyes scanned my surroundings again. The shadows were stretching longer, the sun still bright in my eyes, blinding me and creating opportunity for someone to sneak up on me. Chloe's initial suspicions had gotten to me.

"Well, why did they break up?" Chloe persisted.

"She cheated on him."

"Ah-ha! Well, there you go."

"What?" I wasn't following her train of thought.

"Look, think of it from the ex's side. If a woman were truly, deeply committed to a guy, she wouldn't even dream of cheating on him. But if she wasn't fully invested in the relationship…"

"That's a generalization."

"That is true a lot of the time."

"People cheat for all kinds of reasons."

"One of them being that the relationship had died long before it ended."

I thought about that for a minute. "Yeah, I guess so."

"Think of it long-term."

"How many different ways can I think about it?"

"Oh, I'm sorry," she said. "Are you in a rush right now?" Sarcasm bit at her words and put me in my place.

"Go on."

"In the long-run, the distance thing won't matter. You only have one more semester left of school, and then you graduate. Do you want to move back in with your mother here in Oakfield?"

"No." I wanted to get as far away from her as I could.

"Exactly. And you'll be looking for a job then, too. And since you want to get out of Oakfield anyway, this could be perfect. You'd have so many more marketing job opportunities in New York City than back here."

"And have a lot more competition."

"Sure, but you'd probably also make a lot more money."

"And I'd have to *pay* a lot more money, too," I added.

Chloe sighed. "Are you determined to be pessimistic?"

"No, I'm just not seeing how this could turn out well. You're saying I should marry Brian and move to New York City just so I don't have to move back in with my mother?"

"Whoa, who is talking about marriage?"

I rolled my eyes. "That's what was implied."

"No, what I'm saying is that you clearly like him. And he clearly likes you. A guy doesn't take a stranger on a tour of New York City and risk getting arrested trying to get in the Thanksgiving Day Parade just to be nice. He does it because he likes you. *A lot*."

Damn. Did everyone know of the risk of arrest? And should I feel lucky that I dodged that bullet?

"All I'm saying, Jules, is don't rule him out just because of the distance."

"Yeah…" I muttered noncommittally. I was getting tired of talking about it. Chloe was supposed to be a distraction from Brian.

"Now, getting back to where you're staying

tonight, did you confirm that those people were his *actual* family?" she asked.

I narrowed my eyes, taking another sweep of the street. Still quiet. Either this was a boring part of the city, or Thanksgiving was a bigger commitment than I had given it credit for.

"Who else would they be?"

"Hired actors to fool you."

"So that he could murder me? I don't think so."

"Can't ever be too sure."

"You watch too much TV." I shook my head and remembered the look on Brian's family's faces when I walked through the door and not that Kendra girl. "They were *definitely* his real family. Kids and all."

"Oh, so you'd be an instant aunt," Chloe said.

"I'm not going—"

My phone beeped twice and then cut out. I pulled it away from my ear and stared at it. The screen was blank, except for the line going through the battery symbol on the front, but even that faded after a few seconds.

"Great," I murmured. Now I had no phone. No line to the outside world. No way to book the bus ticket. Maybe I should go to Brian's mother's apartment—if I could even remember where it was—so that I could charge my phone and have a place to stay for the night. And yet, my feet refused to move.

Instead, I sat on the curb, trying not to think about the amount of dirt and grime on the concrete from all the things that people had littered throughout the years. At least there wasn't any stench of garbage, like there had been in other parts of the city.

I felt like an idiot for ruining my holiday—even if that holiday was going to be a sad, miserable experience anyway. I felt even lousier for ruining whatever chances I had with Brian. Chloe was right. He clearly liked me if he went through all that trouble to help me. Why was I even worried about his ex?

My stomach ached with hunger again. I needed to find a place to eat, but I had no money. Maybe they'd at least let me stay in a cafe or something so I could use the bathroom when I needed to. And once I had thought about using the bathroom, of course I felt as though I needed to go.

This was hell.

But didn't I deserve the punishment? I needed a terrible experience to remind me never to let myself be controlled and manipulated by others again. To stop vying for everyone else's approval.

I hugged myself and leaned forward on my knees. The chill was getting to me as the shadows stretched longer. Right now, Brian was probably having turkey with his family. Turkey and cranberry sauce and mashed potatoes and stuffing and later, pie. Pumpkin pie and apple pie and chocolate pie. It all sounded delicious. Especially as my stomach reminded me over and over again that it was empty.

My mom usually undercooked the turkey, risking salmonella poisoning to the whole family every year. And the potatoes were usually cold and the boxed stuffing was sometimes still crunchy. She hated cooking, but everyone else in the house hated her, so nobody offered to help. With that memory, I was almost grateful to be sitting on the sidewalk instead of in my mother's tension-filled house.

Brian's family didn't seem like they argued like mine did. Sure, they probably bickered like every family, but they seemed to love each other. The fact that his mother was already cooking dinner at seven-thirty in the morning was proof that she was a better cook than my mother. And I bet her food tasted great.

If I did make it over to Brian's apartment, things would be awkward, sure, but his family would let me stay. They'd welcome me, try to strike up conversation, and make me feel comfortable. Even if they had been expecting his ex. I envisioned what other holidays were like with his family. Christmas and Easter and birthdays and even Fourth of July parties. Each holiday likely had its own long-held traditions. Each one filled with love and happiness and the good kind of chaos.

I shook my head. My hunger was getting the best of me, making me hallucinate with daydreams that would never happen. I barely knew Brian, and I would never get to know him any more. He was in my past now.

"Excuse me, miss, do you know when the bus is coming?"

The voice behind me sent me into fight-or-flight mode and I jumped to my feet and whipped around with my phone jutting out of the bottom of my hand, aimed for the face of the jerk who thought it would be appropriate to sneak up on me.

Brian's hand went up and deflected the attack, which sent my battery-drained phone clattering to the sidewalk.

As I stared at him, my brain tried to convince the rest of my body that there was no imminent danger. He must've come off the High Line, and with the rattle of the trains going to Penn Station—not to mention the other sounds of the city—I must not have heard him. Still, my heart raced with the fear of the possibilities.

"Oh." I cleared my throat and adjusted my jacket. "It's just you."

He picked up my phone and handed it to me, and that's when I noticed something else.

"You're wearing my purse?"

He readjusted it on his shoulder. "Yeah. I thought it looked better on me."

I cocked an eyebrow, not willing to let down my defenses by smiling, even if I found the remark humorous.

Finally, he slid the bag off his shoulder and handed it to me. "No, dummy, you left it in the trailer back at the park. I figured you'd want it back."

I took it from him and slid it onto my shoulder. "You figured right." Then, as an afterthought, "Thanks."

We fell into an awkward silence, both of us holding onto our pride — what little of it I had left — and not wanting to be the first to apologize. But then, where else would I be if Brian hadn't shown up? Probably trying to find a semi-private corner on the street to pee, and begging people for food until I could find a way back home. And he *had* brought my bag with him, which had my charger and my wallet in it. I didn't *need* to go to Brian's apartment anymore, which meant that I didn't owe him anything.

And yet, we had unfinished business that needed resolving because as much as I tried to talk myself

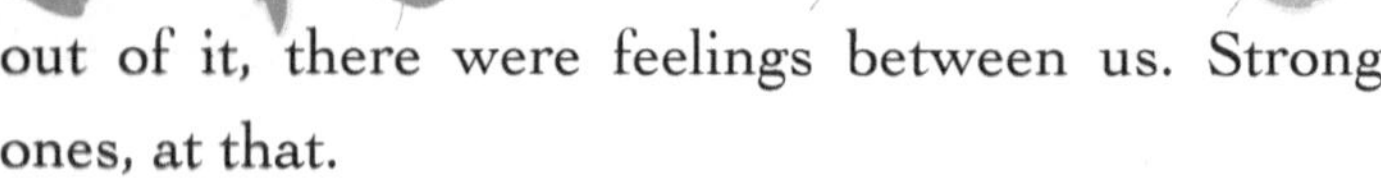

out of it, there were feelings between us. Strong ones, at that.

"Look, Bri—" I started at the same time he did.

"I'm sor—"

He chuckled awkwardly, then gestured to me. "You go first."

"No, you go," I insisted. Somewhere in the confusion, I heard the beginning of the apology from him.

Apparently I still held on to my stubborn pride after all.

"Julie, I'm sorry," he said. "I never meant to make you feel like a rebound. Yes, I did just break up with Kendra last night, but, if I'm being honest, I knew that relationship was over long before it ended. I had given up too much for her and she hadn't been willing to sacrifice very much at all. When I found her in bed with another guy, I knew it was finally over. I mean, of course her cheating was a huge betrayal, and something I need to work through, but it's the betrayal that hurts more, not the break-up. And honestly, what I felt for Kendra doesn't even begin to add up to what I feel for you. And that's a little terrifying."

My eyes widened. Terrifying for us both.

"I couldn't let you leave without laying it out on the table like that," he said. "The truth is, I want to see if we have a future together. I want to see if this thing between us can withstand all the obstacles that are in our way."

I stood frozen to the sidewalk, forgetting the world around us. "But we live so far apart, Brian. And we don't know each other. And—"

Brian took my hands. "If we were together, we would figure it out. We would *both* compromise. If you want to move back home, then I'll find a way to make that work. And if you want to move to Tahiti…well, I'd have to learn where that is."

That stupid little joke is what broke me. I laughed. It was hard not to laugh around him. It was hard to stay mad at him. "Brian, I like you, too," I admitted. "But are we crazy for doing this? For trying to make this work? We just met last night!"

"Of course we're crazy, but that doesn't mean we can't try. All I know is that I want every day to be like this one."

"*Every* day?" I asked. "I don't know. Today was…a lot."

Now he laughed. "Okay, maybe not *quite* like this one, but I want us to be together. I want us to laugh and bicker and *bug* each other every day." He lifted his hand and moved some of my hair out of my face. "Julie, I want to make this work. You came out of nowhere and turned my world around and I can't just

let that go. I can't let *you* go."

I sighed and turned my head away from him, but allowed him to wrap his arms around me. "I want that, too. And lucky for you, moving back to Oakfield permanently is not something I want to do. Not with the way my family is—or my friends from the bar."

"The ones who sent you here? The reason we met?"

Another sigh. "Okay, so they did me *one* favor in all my life. And I'm sure they've done more, but I've realized that I've grown and a lot of them haven't. I'm ready to move on to bigger and better things. Like New York."

He smiled. "Yeah?"

"Of course, I'll still go home to visit, but that's not where I belong. I don't think it's ever where I belonged."

"And you think you belong here?" he asked.

I shrugged. "I don't know. But I'm willing to see. We're doing crazy things now, apparently, right? I'm never going to know unless I give it a shot. The same goes for us. We're just going to keep wondering if this could've worked if we don't at least try."

He kissed me again. "And we'll try. We'll keep trying until it works."

"And if it doesn't?" I asked.

Brian considered that. "If it doesn't end up

working out, then at least we'll have had some good moments. But I don't want to focus on that. I want to focus on how we can make it right."

I gave him a look, but shifted my gaze into a softer one. "I'm sorry for overreacting about your ex. You're allowed to have a past. But I'm not looking for a fling."

"Neither am I."

"I mean it. Across the board, I've realized that I've been surrounding myself with shallow people and I'm tired of it. I need something more. I need something deeper. More meaningful. If the two of us even stand a shot, you have to know that that's what I'm looking for."

"So am I." He leaned in and kissed me.

We wrapped our arms around each other, which reminded me of something else.

"Did your family eat all of the turkey?" I asked.

"I don't know. I'm sure there's some left. Why?"

"I'm *starving*!"

He hooked his arm around my shoulder and led me in the direction of the subway. "Then let's get that taken care of. I'm a little famished myself."

"And are there any coffee shops or corner stores open?"

"Probably. Why? You can't wait until we get back to my apartment?"

"No, I really have to pee!"

Some marching band drummed on the TV while I fussed with the potatoes in the kitchen. I still wasn't much of a cook, but I had learned a lot since making a concerted effort to learn. Thanksgiving was a special time, especially for me and Brian, and I wanted to signify that this year by making him a full Thanksgiving feast.

I had also called his mother twelve times in the last two hours. Luckily, she had been more than willing to help since I was preparing the feast this year and not her.

Part of the struggle of preparing the feast was that we didn't have all the right kitchen utensils yet. One of them being an electric mixer, which meant that I was hand-mashing the potatoes while simultaneously scrolling my phone and occasionally looking up at the TV.

Okay, so I probably shouldn't have been multi-tasking, but I was reading the comments on my latest post. A two-year reflection on my relationship with Brian.

The viral post I had been looking for came with that spontaneous trip to New York City. But it hadn't been the multitude of videos I had taken trying to get in the parade that had blown up. Instead, it was the unlikely love story that bloomed between the two of us. The first glances, feelings of butterflies, and easy candor that was all caught while trying to capture something else.

I had compiled all those special moments and wrote a long, heart-felt caption about our journey and It. Blew. Up.

My follower count shot through the roof on all of my social media accounts, which led to multiple job offers across the country. Who needs college anyway? Companies saw how many followers I had and the type of content that I had on my pages and wanted to hire me to manage their own social media accounts.

Of course, in the end, I had chosen a job in New York City so that I could be with Brian. I was now the Marketing Coordinator at NYU, where Brian also worked.

I looked down at the potatoes and determined that they were sufficiently mashed. After banging the masher on the side of the bowl to knock off the rest of the potatoes, I tossed the utensil in the growing pile of dishes in the sink, then carried the bowl over to the dining room table, which had a view of the park.

When Brian lived in Canada, he had been working remotely for NYU, but moving back to New York had allowed him to be in the right place at the right time—or maybe he was just more on the radar of his bosses since he was in the office—and he got a huge promotion within the admissions department.

That, coupled with my new job at the same institution, allowed us to get our own apartment. One that had a beautiful view of the park. I wasn't going to pretend like that view would be around forever—with the way the super tall towers were going up around Central Park, our precious view was bound to have an end date. But for the moment, it allowed us to remember where our love story began.

In the next room, the vacuum turned off and Brian came out with it in his hand. When he saw me, he smiled and set the vacuum aside, taking the opportunity to wrap his arms around me from behind and kiss my neck.

I flinched and laughed as his skin grazed against mine. "Is the house all clean?"

"Yep. How's dinner coming? It smells delicious."

"It's coming along." I held his interlocked hands against my belly and leaned back into him. His touch was still comforting, just like it had been the first time he held me. "Don't expect perfection. I'm not your mother."

He pulled away, then came around to face me. "Eh, my mother wasn't perfect her first time making Thanksgiving dinner, either. Even after that, I remember so many times that she'd burn the biscuits or left the mashed potatoes lumpy."

I thought about the potatoes. Did I mash them enough? But then I thought about the similarities between his mother's cooking mishaps and my own mother's mishaps. They had made the same mistakes. The difference was, Brian's mother laughed it off and created a funny family memory, while mine had created a moment of tension.

Good thing I wasn't cooking for my mother. She and I really only exchanged phone calls a couple times a year. Completely out of obligation. Neither one of us knew what to say to each other.

"Do you need help with anything?" Brian asked.

I laughed. "No, thank you. I will gladly cook the whole meal myself." The deal had been, if I spent all day cooking, he spent all day cleaning. From vacuuming to toilets to dishes, I definitely got the better end of the deal.

"Okay, I suppose that's fair," he said with a chuckle. "Can't blame a guy for trying."

I leaned in and kissed him. Mostly because I could. Because I felt like it. And when I pulled away, I saw him get a different idea in his head, and with the turkey in the oven and a whole list of other things to get done, we didn't have time for it.

"What time is your family coming?" I asked as a way to distract him.

"In about an hour."

My eyes widened. "An hour! Oh, wow, I still have a lot to do." The turkey needed to be pulled out and carved, the biscuits needed to be baked, the gravy heated up, the table set. Not to mention that I still had to take a shower and get myself dressed. It was all doable, but it would take the full hour.

"It's okay if you're still cooking when they come," he assured me. "My mother will probably volunteer to help, and so will Tina and Rebecca."

I let out a heavy sigh. "I know that."

"Will this help set you at ease?"

My brow furrowed, not sure of what he meant. And then he dropped down to his knee and pulled a small box out of his pocket.

It was happening. The moment that had been hyped up in every romance story. The proposal.

And it was completely unexpected.

Sure, it was Thanksgiving, our anniversary. It was in our apartment, in front of the window overlooking the park. But I still had no idea it was coming.

I had flour smeared on my clothes and my hair was a mess and the house smelled delicious and the vacuum clunked to the floor…

And yet…it was perfect. Brian was perfect. Or, at least, perfect for me. For my own brand of craziness. Perfectly matched my wild ideas. Someone to help ease my tortured soul. And I was perfect for him and all of his scars and baggage that he had been sorting through over the last two years, learning how to undo and relearn his patterns with romantic relationships.

It was ours. And I wanted to hold onto it forever. And, apparently, so did Brian.

"Julie, will you marry me?" he asked.

I beamed. "Yes, of course!"

And I knew, from that moment on, that Thanksgiving would forever hold a special place in our hearts.

Behind the Book:
Thanksgiving Day
PARADE

This book came out of nowhere.

I wasn't planning on writing it. I never thought I'd have a Thanksgiving book. I never thought I'd have any romance books outside of the Christmas theme. And yet here you are, sitting at the end of this book, having (hopefully) enjoyed it.

So what happened?

Every year I binge Christmas romance reads throughout November and December. I like them, but it's also a way for me to get inspiration for more Christmas book ideas myself.

Well, at the end of 2023, I was feeling pretty happy about the week of Thanksgiving specifically. I work at a school and that Monday and Tuesday are technically work days, but they're also no-student days. If you're a teacher you know that any time the staff needs to report and the students don't, it's practically like a day off. You get so much stuff done! Think of it like sending your kids to daycare and spending the first hour picking up your house without interruptions.

Bliss.

Anyway, that Tuesday the staff usually does a Thanksgiving feast where we all bring a dish to pass and sit together and enjoy a home-cooked meal. It's a lot of fun.

So I was pretty excited for that, but also, now that I'm an adult, a new tradition has sprung up with my mother and grandmother. Instead of them struggling to find something for me for Christmas, we go Christmas shopping ahead of time where I pick out clothes that I want and they wrap it up for me for Christmas. It's a win-win because I get what I want, but we also get to spend an extra day together. Lately, we've been doing that the day before Thanksgiving because everyone has off that day and the Black Friday deals last all week now.

Thanksgiving Day itself is also fun because there is a lot less pressure to "prepare" for the holiday ahead of time. Don't get me wrong, I love Christmas and everything that goes into making it happen, but wow is it a lot of work! It's like having a part-time job on top of everything else for the month of December!

Black Friday my brothers and I go bowling and out to lunch. Now that we have kids, our group has expanded, but it's still fun.

All that to say, the week of Thanksgiving has a lot to look forward to. So in 2023, I was looking to also read a Thanksgiving book…and the only one I could find was Janet Evanovich's *Thanksgiving*.

Bought it. Read it. Enjoyed it.

But then it got me thinking, why aren't there more Thanksgiving stories? And that's where the ideas for *Thanksgiving Day Parade* started to spring up.

In fact, I was so inspired that I plotted out the book in between writing the first draft of A Christmas Family. And then, since I had other writing commitments, that outline sat on my computer for months and I ended up writing the first draft of this book in May/June of 2024. There was even a week where we had 90 degree weather and I was writing about Thanksgiving and feeling a nip in the air.

The end result turned out to be something I really enjoyed working on. I can always tell when a book is special when I feel so completely immersed in the world and know the characters inside and out. I looked forward to writing this book and now I'm inspired to write more romances outside of the Christmas theme.

If you enjoyed this book, please leave a review online! Reviews help future readers decide whether to give a book a shot. Who knows? Your review might help someone find their next favorite read!

Thanks for reading!

If you liked this book, pick up
A Christmas Reunion, another sweet
romance book!

DavidNethBooks.com/
SmallTownChristmas

I'll be home for Christmas…

Tracy Slater may be a successful pop star, but fame and fortune isn't everything she thought it'd be. Under the thumb of a husband who is growing steadily more abusive, she's decided her marriage is over. She just needs to make it through one more trip home for the holidays with him before she's free.

If only in my dreams…

Stephen Austin worked hard to become the successful novelist he's always wanted to be. So why isn't he happy? And why does he feel so lonely? Then he runs into his old girlfriend, the one he thought he had lost forever.

Tormented by the mistakes of their past, Stephen sees his reunion with Tracy as a second chance. But does she feel the same way?

A Christmas Reunion is the first book in the Small Town Christmas series. Each book in the series is an independent story and the series can be read in any order.

A Christmas Reunion

A Novella

—Small Town Christmas—
Book 1

D. Allen

Chapter One
TRACY

DECEMBER 20TH

As my driver pulls into the airport, I worry that I made the wrong decision about coming home. There's just too much work to do. I'm not even going back to my place in LA since the press tour ended for the new album. I'm flying right from New York to Batavia. Charlie doesn't like it.

"Why don't I just go back to check in on things? I'll meet you back at your mom's place in a couple days," he pleaded last night.

"What am I supposed to tell Mom when I show up without my husband?" I retorted. Mom's always worried that I don't make enough time for family. She says I work too hard.

And now Charlie has refused to talk to me all day.

He stayed back at the hotel while I hit the gym this morning and met with my team at the label one last time before the holidays. He took the last few weeks off from work, claiming we'd be able to spend it together. Obviously he didn't pay attention the millions of times I told him that I had to work up until the third week of December.

What's really set him off is where the argument turned last night. Where it *always* turns: kids. He says he doesn't want to be in his sixties when our kids are just graduating high school.

The airport is crowded when Charlie and I enter. Typical of the holiday season, but before we even reach security, a group of girls stops us to get my autograph and take some pictures.

Charlie stands off to the side and flashes me his phone to show the time. No matter where I am I try to make time for anyone who approaches me for a picture. Charlie usually tells me to politely decline if I'm in a rush. He's not a fan of my career. He thinks that I should stop working at this "silly singing thing" and focus on being a mother.

Yeah, like he doesn't enjoy the private jet and the $3 million house this "silly singing thing" pays for. Not to mention his wardrobe of designer suits that he wears to impress his colleagues. I'm sure they know that I'm the real moneymaker in our marriage. That's gotta be a blow to his fragile masculinity.

Just as the last of the girls is snapping a selfie of us on her phone, Charlie grabs my elbow and says, "Honey, we have a flight to catch."

After security we use a special exit that takes us onto the runway to board the private jet. It's equipped with the works—leather seats, kitchenette, TVs, you name it. It's practically a flying house.

"That was rude," I mutter as I take my seat.

"You're the one who is in such a rush to get home." He takes the seat behind me, which I don't question. We haven't really talked since last night's argument—not that we usually do—and emotions are still high.

Hopefully going to my mom's will alleviate some of the tension. Based on previous holidays and family gatherings, I know that as soon as we get to the front door, he'll turn on his charm and act like the proud, doting husband that he has everyone believing he is.

After I told my mom I was coming home for Christmas, she immediately told me about Daisy Doyle's grand idea to throw a holiday class reunion. I guess her married name is Daniels—still got those double Ds. Her husband has to be deaf. Or blind. Or both.

No, Daisy's not the worst person I've met. When you mingle with entitled celebrities and name-droppers, your faith in humanity pretty much goes out the window. Daisy's just…intense sometimes. Or at least she was the last time I saw her ten years ago.

She wants me to sing something at the reunion. I don't even want to go. We'll see. It's supposed to be a pre-Christmas mixer to catch folks who are in town for the holidays. Everyone else probably already has plans for that day, so it's likely to be a dud. Maybe I can talk her out of having me sing.

It's not that I dislike singing. I love it. Obviously, I've made a career out of it. It's just that I've escalated into a different world than everyone else. "Show business." Singing will only shove my success in their faces and further prove that I'm different. That I no longer fit in with the rest of them.

Still, there are a few people I wouldn't mind catching up with. People I haven't seen since graduation. I had a lot of fun in high school. Besides my family, there isn't really anyone from back home that I still talk to, which is a shame.

I look out the window as the plane rises above the city. The lights beneath are beautiful. Mom would likely be trying to take a million pictures. Of course, she would have to ask for someone's help to find her camera app, then she'd complain about the glare from the window. I can't help but smile at that.

D. ALLEN

I'm anxious to see my mom. Since Dad died, her health has been slipping. Complications from her diabetes and congestive heart failure. My guess is she hasn't been watching her diet like she's supposed to. My sister, Kimmy, checks on her as often as she can, but she's married with two kids of her own. She's busy. I'm busy. So busy I can't even *call* my mother every week. I'm hoping this visit will help with some of that neglect.

The plane lands an hour or so later at the small county airport just outside the city. If you would've told me as a teenager that I'd be using it with my own private jet, I never would've believed you. But then, I never would've been able to predict any part of my adult life.

The brisk December wind hits me as Charlie and I descend the stairs onto the runway. My hair flies in my face and I don't notice my sister at first as she approaches, but I definitely hear her loud scream when she spots me.

A wide grin stretches across my face. Someone genuinely happy to see me for me, not just my accomplishments? I immediately feel at home. Besides, she's my big sister. Even though I'm extremely busy, I've managed to keep in touch with her through texts and the random tagging on Facebook.

"Oh, I've missed you so much!" she nearly shouts in my ear over the roar of the wind and the plane. She squeezes me as tight as she can in our puffy coats.

"I've missed you too!" I hold her out at arm's length. "You look so good! Did you cut your hair?"

Kimmy might as well be the antithesis of me. She has short-cropped brunette hair, I have long blonde hair—now platinum blonde due to my stylist determining I need a "bold" look. While she's always supported my career, she would never even think of pursuing the same profession. Too much detail on perfection, too much focus on beauty, too much exposure, too much time.

Besides, Kimmy's purpose in life has always been motherhood. Even before she had kids, she was always the more responsible one. The one to sacrifice her free time to make sure I got to class or practice on time. The one who treated our pets as her babies. Being a celebrity doesn't allow for time to start a family. Especially not when you're "Tracy Slater."

Kimmy reaches back and pats her bare neck. "Yeah. Do you think it's too much?"

"No!" I exclaim. "I think you should put a hat on in this weather, but it looks cute!"

My sister and husband exchange polite nods, but her attention returns to me.

Some of the airport staff usher us into the terminal, where Charlie finally speaks up. He goes in for an awkward hug with Kimmy and says, "It's good to see you. You guys should come out to California sometime with the kids."

Yet another reason why we're not ready to have kids. Charlie just doesn't get it.

It's not like we don't have the room for my sister and her family. I would love to have her. It's just not feasible. Besides, what would the kids *do* at our house? Sure, we have the pool, but I just know Charlie will throw a fit when they start tracking the water inside the house or knocking too much of it out. And all of our "art"? Consider those gone, Chuckie.

My sister must sense my mood and politely smiles at my husband. "Maybe this summer we can meet up with you guys on tour. I know the boys loved it when Trace brought them on stage with the last one."

"Right. Yeah." The mention of my upcoming work obligations causes him to lose interest.

"Do we have everything?" I ask.

Normally my assistant would be on top of moving the schedule along—even if it's a vacation—but I gave her the rest of the year off. I already felt guilty for having her work so late into December. Usually I give her the whole month off, but the label wanted to push Black Friday and pre-Christmas sales, meaning press got bumped closer to the holidays.

A Christmas Reunion

"Yeah." Charlie grabs our bags and heads to the door to the parking lot.

Kimmy brings her eyebrows together and I roll my eyes in response.

* * *

Nothing can quite compare to sitting in my childhood home decorated for Christmas with the fire crackling and the likes of Nat "King" Cole, Dean Martin, and Brenda Lee playing softly in the background. Add my mother's turkey casserole—likely made from leftover Thanksgiving fixings—and you have the perfect evening.

My sister couldn't stay for dinner. Her oldest son was in his first school play: *A Christmas Carol.* I guess he insisted that his parents go to all three showings. My mom went last night. Tonight is the final night, and I would've liked to go, but I didn't even bring it up. I knew Charlie would make a face and grumble the whole time. For someone who claims to want kids, he doesn't have a lot of tolerance for them.

Not to mention I still need to prepare myself to see everyone. Returning to my former high school in one of my camera-ready outfits is not what I want to do. I purposely packed jeans and modest sweaters to help blend in. I'm not here to upstage anyone.

"Has Daisy talked to you yet?" Mom asks as she pulls the casserole out of the oven.

I fuss with the corner of the forest-green placemat. "Sort of. I've e-mailed her a few times. She's mostly talked to Missy since I've been so busy with the album drop and everything."

"Missy?"

"My assistant."

"Oh." Mom nods. She begins dishing out our plates.

"Do you need any help, Mom?" Charlie asks. *Mom*? That's new.

She smiles. "No, dear, I've got it all under control. You two just take a seat."

Charlie sits back with a smug smile on his face.

When Mom joins us at the table, she continues, "You really should give Daisy a call. She's so happy you're back in town for a bit. She says everyone who's coming to the mixer is excited to see you."

"She told everyone I'm coming?" I groan.

"Well yeah, sweetie. They'll be happy to see you. Why are you upset?"

I shrug. "I don't know." I poke around my plate with my fork. It's not worth it to go into how people expect to see "Tracy Slater," the celebrity, when all I want to be while I'm home is just Tracy, the old high school friend.

Charlie doesn't like it when I talk about the two sides of myself. Apparently it's bogus and I'm just fishing for attention. He doesn't get it. Not like he used to. When we first got together, I felt like he knew everything about me. Of course, we only dated while I was on tour and married shortly after it ended. I suppose it was like summer camp. It worked when we made a special effort to see each other, but now that we're married and have two very different careers, it's just not the same.

"I've got her number by the phone. Give her a call. Oh, not tonight, though. She's in charge of the school play."

I give a tight smile. "Of course she is."

"It's a shame we missed the play," Charlie says. He taps his plate with his fork. "This is very good. Thanks for making it."

I look down at my plate and roll my eyes. What an act.

"Oh, I'm glad you like it!" Mom smiles. "The play was cute. Maybe someday soon you two will be going for your kid."

"Mom!"

"That would be nice," Charlie adds.

"Tracy, you're not getting any younger. Trust me, I

D. ALLEN

was older when I had you girls, and there were certainly challenges. Look at me now! I may never get to see grandchildren from you."

"Don't say that!"

She shrugs. "I'm just saying…"

Charlie nods and looks at me.

I bite my lip and look away.

Mom gets up, grabs something from the counter, and hands it to me. It's one of the magazine covers I did. I haven't seen it yet, so it must've just come out.

"Tracy, I think it's great that you're doing so well, and you know how proud I am of you, but look at that. I'm just worried that you won't have any maternal instincts left if you keep things like this up."

I study the cover and try to determine what she's taken offense with. It's not one of my sultrier poses that she usually condemns. I'm actually smiling in this one!

"What is it?" I finally ask.

"Is there even a reason for you to be wearing a top if you're going to show off the girls anyway?" She shoves her hands under her breasts and gives a little shake. Not what I expected from a woman wearing a sweater with kittens in Santa hats.

My top in the picture is cut lower than I'm used to wearing, but it's still pretty modest compared to most magazine covers. Besides, compared to other pop stars,

I'm a saint. But based on the look on my mother's face, I look like a whore.

Charlie glances over. "Mmm, you're right. I don't know if I would've approved of that one if I were there."

I glare at him. First of all, he doesn't *approve* of anything I wear. Second, he *was* there, and I'm pretty sure he was drooling at some of the pictures that were taken. I believe he told me later that I don't fix myself up for him like I do for the camera. And yet, he's stumped why we don't have more sex.

I toss the magazine back on the table. "Mom, these covers are all digitally modified."

"And you're okay with that? What if they changed it so you were naked on the cover?"

"Well, they can't do *that*."

"Then why didn't you ask to see the final photos?"

"If I asked to see the final photos for every picture that's taken of me, I'd never get anything else done!"

"I agree with your mother," Charlie cuts in. "You need to be careful about what you're putting out for the world to see. Our future kids will be seeing things like this eventually."

Mom nods.

"Charlie…" I growl between my teeth.

He knows. He knows exactly what circumstances I'm in. He knows how busy I am and how carefully I put together my brand. Showing some cleavage doesn't ruin that. I know what I'm doing. I've been doing it for years. Besides, my children—if I decide to have them—will know how to respect women.

But if he agrees with me, he can't play up to my mother's expectations of being the perfect son-in-law. I know she sees through the ruse sometimes, but other times I can't believe how gullible she is.

My mother's objections to some of my career choices don't bother me. She usually nitpicks the little things, but I know she's proud of the big things. It seems like she takes an ad out in the paper every time I win an award. And to my knowledge, she's never missed one of my performances on TV—thanks to Kimmy showing her how to use the DVR. She's definitely always been cheering me on, even if she has an opinion on some things.

What bothers me is my husband's complete abandonment of support whenever it suits him. Sometimes I wish he would just go away.

❄ ❄ ❄

My old bedroom is now a guest room. The flowery wallpaper remains, as well as the spot by the closet door that I had used as a coloring canvas when I was six. I remember my mother scrubbing at it for a long time, working away the colorful wax. It still stained the paper, leaving an odd salmon color.

It's a small room for a double bed, but without any other furniture besides a dresser and an end table, it works. What I'm not looking forward to is sharing such a tight space with Charlie. At home we have a king size, so I can pretty much put as much space between us as I need. Besides, our work schedules differ so much we barely spend any time together in the same bed.

"You seemed awfully chummy with my mom," I say as I unload my clothes into the dresser.

"And you seemed awfully pissy." He lies against the headboard, his eyes on his phone.

"At least I'm not putting on a show for everyone."

"It's what you do every day. You should be used to it. What did you tell me? There are two versions of you? Which version am I getting now?"

I slam the dresser shut. "Never mind. You obviously don't get it." I try to walk by him and out the door, but he grabs ahold of my arm.

"Hey, come here." He stands and pulls me into a hug. He has my arms pinned to my side, making it impossible to return it. "Just try to lighten up. It is the holidays, after all."

He leans in for a kiss, but I back away.

D. ALLEN

"Lighten up? I'm not the one ruining everyone's time."

"Really? You're ruining my time."

"Maybe that's your problem, then."

He overturns his hands. "I think you're the one with the problem. What's the matter? You've been short with me ever since we got here. Before that, even."

I cross my arms and glare at him. "Do you really want to do this now?"

"If it's the only time I can get you to open up, then yes. Let's do this now."

I study him, trying to decipher whether he knows what I'm thinking. This relationship has turned hostile in the last year. I've lost an unhealthy amount of weight. His anger has been growing steadily, not to mention his back acne. Add the cost of his dermatologist and expensive zit cream to the tab of his sugar mama.

"This isn't working anymore."

He looks confused. Clearly we're not on the same page. Either that or he's playing dumb to make me look like the bitch. Wouldn't be the first time.

"What are you talking about?" he asks.

"I want a divorce."

"What?"

I shrug. "Or a separation or something. Maybe see a counselor until we figure it out. But for the time being, you and I can't solve our problems on our own."

He shakes his head. "No, we're not separating. I'm not divorcing you."

"Okay, so *I'll* divorce *you*. If I want to end the marriage, there's really nothing you can do about it." That last bit of information came straight from an attorney I've already got on retainer.

"No."

I squint my eyes at him. "No?"

"Little Miss Tracy Slater is going to get over herself and actually think about someone else for a change. It's time you showed me a little respect."

"Respect?" I fight to keep my voice down. "Charlie, you constantly discredit my accomplishments."

He rolls his eyes. "Please, you're not curing cancer."

"And you are?" He's an investment banker. Basically, shifting money around. Back when I met him, he was my reminder than real people have day jobs. That, and the label loved that his company was always willing to sponsor my shows.

"That's enough. Now let's put on a happy smile and go enjoy the holidays with your mother, which you insisted on."

"I never get to see her, Charlie!" I whisper-shout. "None of my family. I think I deserve to spend a week with them for Christmas."

"And what about my family? You don't think I want to see them?"

"We just saw them for Thanksgiving! Not to mention the cruise we went on last summer with your brother, or don't you remember the private yacht you insisted I pay half for?"

"*We* paid half for!"

"That's funny, because I'm pretty sure the cash came out of *my* account."

"*Our* account."

"You can say that all you want, but I still make more than you, and that's a fact you can't stand."

I'm thrown onto the small bed, his finger in my face.

"Just because you sell yourself out like a cheap whore doesn't mean you can throw it in my face!"

I stare at him, my heart pounding in my chest.

He balls his fist near my face. "And you keep your mouth shut about this divorce business."

I watch as he leaves, still frozen in place. My heart races. I hate that man. I want him gone. But in this tiny bedroom and with the approaching holiday, I'm trapped.

Chapter Two
STEPHEN

DECEMBER 20TH

I find myself at the bar on Jackson Street again tonight. The muse just isn't with me. Hasn't been in a while. Sometimes I wonder if the height of my career—and my life—is behind me. The magic lost.

Three bestselling books and several other critically acclaimed and fan-favorite books have graced my writing career, but the well has run dry. My publisher pesters me every week for something new. I haven't put out a new book in almost two years. Haven't written anything decent in just about six months.

Of course, it doesn't help that whenever I hear from my editor, she's always saying things like, "Can't wait to read what you've cooked up next!" or "If your previous books are any indication, we're all in for a real treat!"

Despite not writing a single thing today, my shoulders are knotted with stress. I need to unwind. The weight of failure sits heavy on me, making it even harder to finally write the story I intend to.

The bartender is new. His plain white T-shirt almost seems to bring out the baby fat he still has on his cheeks. Despite his recent employment, I've been coming here so frequently lately that he doesn't have to ask what I want. The bottle's at my usual spot before I even sit down.

"Thanks," I say before I take my first sip.

He wipes the bar with a rag. "You went to school here in town, right?"

I nod.

He pulls a flyer from the wall behind the bar and sets it beside me. "This your class?"

It's an announcement for my ten-year class reunion. The preholiday "mixer" is here. They rent out the restaurant part of the bar now and then for private events.

I've seen the flyers. I got the e-mails.

"Yeah, that's me."

"You going?"

I shake my head. "Probably not."

D. Allen

He shrugs. "Could be fun. Compare how well you're doing to how your former classmates are."

I roll my eyes. "I didn't like them in high school. I'm not going to like them now." I push the flyer away. "Remind me to stay away that night."

He pins it back on the wall and lets me have my space for a while. I read the news headlines on the TV above the liquor display.

"Hank tells me you're a writer."

I snort in response. "Sort of."

"Have you written anything recently?"

I shake my head now and sip my drink.

"Writer's block?"

I nod. "More like loss of talent."

He busies himself with dusting the liquor bottles on the shelves behind him. It's a Wednesday. A slow night.

"I wouldn't go that far," he says. "You'll figure something out."

I brush him off. He doesn't know the story. He doesn't know me. He's still young and naïve. Thinks everything will work out in the end. Well I've been to the end. I know that life doesn't always have a happily ever after. Not like the ones I'm known for writing.

It's funny, but if my readers actually knew who the real G.W. Austin was, they likely wouldn't buy my books. Not just because I'm a man, but because I'm a talentless drunk. Nothing like the swoon-worthy men I write about. God, sometimes I hate myself. I'm a sellout.

"What kind of books do you write, anyway?" the newbie asks. If Hank were here, he'd know to leave me the hell alone by now.

I give him the benefit of the doubt and decide to humor him. "Funnily enough, romance. I started out writing mysteries. The ones with the heavy romance backstories took off. My editor said I had a knack for writing about people in love. Once I wrote a straight-up romance, the publisher didn't want anything else from me." I shrug. "It sells."

"So what's the problem, then?"

"There's nothing left."

He can't be much older than twenty-one, twenty-two at most. A kid. He scrunches his face in confusion.

"I'm not writing," I add. "The inspiration is gone. Whatever I come up with sucks. New York's never gonna buy that. The characters are forced, the vocabulary is juvenile. I just can't write a believable romance anymore. Starting from scratch with a new genre will result in my reputation being destroyed. Poof! Gone."

My words are crueler than I intend, but the kid doesn't seem to take offense. Working in a bar will do that to you, I guess.

D. ALLEN

He places the bottle of whiskey he finished dusting back on the shelf. "You ever been in love yourself? Maybe that's the problem."

I finish off my drink. "Have I ever been in love? Sure. Once." I pull a ten out of my wallet and set it on the bar. This wasn't as relaxing as I thought it'd be. I'm not about to talk about my feelings to the local barkeep. This isn't a fucking romance novel. Then again, a scene like that would probably end up in the crap I've come up with lately. "That was a long time ago, kid. I'll see you around."

The brisk cold air hits me when I walk outside. Burying my hands in my pockets, I set off for the walk back to my house. It's not far. Maybe ten minutes. As I turn the corner onto Main Street, I nearly collide with two women.

"Oh, I'm sorr—Tracy?"

"Steve?" Her face lights up, and she takes me in for a moment before she reaches up for a hug. "How are you?" she says into my shoulder.

I quickly pat her back and pull away. Returning my hands to my pockets, I say, "Good. I didn't know you were home. It's, uh—"

She nods. "Yeah, it's…" There's a smile on her face, but she doesn't seem to know where to look.

Neither do I. Our footprints in the snow and the

ice collecting on the edge of the street suddenly have my interest.

This is Tracy. My Tracy. Right in front of me. "It's good to see you."

"Yeah, I just got in tonight. I'm—"

"You staying with your sister?" I interrupt. "Sorry, you go."

She smiles and looks down. "No."

"My house is too crazy with the kids," Kimmy adds. I've almost forgotten she's there.

"Right."

"You still live here in town?" Tracy asks.

As hard as I try, I can't keep the smile from my face. "Yup. Over on Summit."

She nods. "Gotcha. I'm staying with my mother for the holidays. We should catch up sometime before I leave. Maybe get some coffee or something?"

"Yeah, I'd like that." I hold her gaze for a while. I divert my eyes to the ground and kick the snow off my sneakers on the sidewalk. "Well, I've gotta get going."

"Right. Me too. We're going to grab something to eat. It was good seeing you."

"You too." I look to her sister. "Nice to see you again, Kimmy."

"Steve," she says with a nod.

During my walk home I'm numb for reasons

completely unrelated to the weather. That was the one and only Tracy Slater. The source of all the emotion I put into my books—or used to. The love of my life in high school. The girl I tried my hardest to get over. For a while I thought I had. And then she began popping up on TV and the radio, and I couldn't escape her or the perfect life she'd created for herself.

But still, I know I'll have a hard time getting her out of my head. She was my world. Things like that don't just go away. Especially when I have nothing to show for my life. No wife, no girlfriend, no kids. Just me.

I have no intention of catching up with her. It wouldn't do me any good. She's moved on. She's married. She has a life out in California. I'm just a memory to her.

Chapter Three
TRACY

DECEMBER 21ST

I'm sitting outside the Tim Horton's on Main Street. I have to talk myself up before I can go inside. Suddenly the apps on my phone require immediate, thorough attention. The low murmur of Christmas music coming from the speakers is the only thing that fills the air.

Daisy wanted to see me "right away" to discuss the possibility of me singing at the mixer. I'm only here to talk her out of it. Well, that's not the only reason. I needed to get out of the house. Mom went to pick up some last-minute gifts, so it was just me and Charlie. At the moment, Daisy is the lesser of two evils.

With a deep breath, I put on my big girl pants and step out into the cold. Inside, Daisy has already claimed a table. She calls my name from across the small café when she sees me and waves her hand in the air. She's wearing a red sweater and jeans. From what I can tell, she's kept in shape. But then, it's only our ten-year reunion. For the most part, everyone still has their youth. Just look at me and how much I'm exploiting it.

I wait in line to grab a cup of tea and head over to Daisy's table. She hugs me like we're old friends, not keeping her voice down at all. Announcing to the world that she's chummy with "Tracy Slater."

It's funny, because the people in the café likely wouldn't believe I am who I am just by looking at me. Or they just plain don't care. I'm not in my stage clothes. I'm not dressed for a photo shoot. I'm dressed for a trip to the coffee shop. In my black peacoat with my hair pulled back, I'm a normal person. That's part of the reason why I needed this trip. To get back in touch with reality.

"Oh my God, so how have you been?" She bends like a pretzel in her seat, legs crossed, leaning on her palm, eyes wide, and ready for any pop star story I might have for her.

"I'm doing okay." I'm not about to name-drop. "Just released the new record, so up until I got in last night, I haven't really had a chance to unwind from the press tour and everything else. I'm ready to just relax."

"I know! You've been all over the place, girl. I *love*

the new album. 'Bittersweet Memories' is probably my favorite. And it's great because I can listen to your stuff with the kids in the car." She puts her hand in front of me on the table and sits back. "Oh my God! You *have* to sign something for my niece! I would be *the* best aunt ever! Mine are still too young, but Abby *loves* you!"

I take a sip of my tea. I should've gotten coffee. Black. Better yet, vodka.

"How old is she?"

"Thirteen. You are her favorite. She doesn't believe me when I tell her we were friends in high school."

"Thirteen." I groan. "You couldn't pay me enough to go back to thirteen."

"Ugh, I know! But it's not like you have money trouble." She laughs loudly.

"Luckily, that's all behind us." I sidestep the money comment. "I know a lot of people probably don't even want to come to this reunion because of all the bad memories." If my media training taught me anything, it was how to steer a conversation back to the point of the meeting.

"Right? That's, like, what I'm afraid of. That nobody will show." Another exaggerated groan. "But I've got flyers *everywhere*. People will come. It's just one night! It's not like we have to relive high school all over again! Wouldn't that be the worst? Ugh!" She giggles loudly, and for just a minute, I feel like I really am back in high school.

"Yeah, I'm sure people will come. I'll be there." Guess that decides that, then. "Even if it's only a few people, it'll be more of an intimate gathering than a big party. The real reunion isn't until this summer, right?"

"Oh yeah! I want to do a couple get-togethers. You know, just to try to coincide with everyone's busy schedules. If you can't make it to one, you can make it to the other. Do you think you'll be coming this summer?"

I grit my teeth. "Oh, I don't know. I'll probably be in the middle of tour. We're still finalizing dates. It really depends on if I have a show and where I am."

"Well that's a bummer." She pulls out a folder and spreads it flat on the table. Slipping a piece of paper from one of the pockets, she pulls out a pen and says, "That's why you need to sing something for this mixer. Give everyone from high school a run for their money, huh?" She laughs in almost that Janice from *Friends* laugh, and I swear it's worse than when I get the high-pitched feedback in my in-ears on tour.

"Yeah, I actually wanted to talk to you about that…"

She doesn't hear me. "So I was thinking we could do a mix at the mixer." Another laugh. God help me. People are staring now, and it has nothing to do with my fame. "I've heard your Christmas EP and it was, *ugh*, beautiful! You have to sing a few things from that! But then I was thinking that people might be getting sick of Christmas songs by now, so you'll need to sing some of your other hits, too. 'Someday' or 'When Will You Be Mine?' or something like that. The big ones, you know?"

"Daisy, I don't really feel comfortable singing at the event."

Her face drops. "Why not?"

"Well, for one, I don't even have my band with me or any of the other equipment we'd need."

She waves a limp hand at me. "That's okay. Maybe just a few a cappella numbers. You could do 'Silent Night' or 'Have Yourself a Merry Little Christmas.' People love those. They're classics. Besides, you've got the voice for it. Of course, we'll have to narrow it down a bit. One or two—"

"That's not...singing is what I do for a living. It's work. I love it, but when I'm meeting up with old friends, I don't want to have to worry about all that. I'm sorry. I'll help in any other way I can, but I don't want to sing."

Daisy lets out an exaggerated breath of air. "Okay. I suppose that's fair. You *are* on vacation, after all. I forget that this isn't home for you anymore."

That hits me harder than I expect it to. This will always be home. But have I been treating it like that?

Not really. I've neglected this town and the people in it since I first saw success. Maybe, against all my efforts not to, I've become a diva so far separated from reality that I can't even identify what really matters anymore.

She closes her folder and sits back, cradling her drink. "Well, I pretty much have everything else figured out. You could come early and help set up, but I mostly wanted to talk to you about what you were going to sing."

I cringe. "Sorry."

Another limp wrist wave. "Don't worry about it. It's okay. It's not like I announced it. I just thought it'd be a nice surprise."

Shrugging, I admit, "Yeah, it would've been."

"Who are you most anxious to see?"

"Me? I don't know." I'm not positive what she implies by "anxious." "Everyone, I guess. I don't really talk to people from high school anymore, so it'll be nice to see everyone."

Daisy rolls her eyes. "Stop being polite! Come on, just between girlfriends, who is it?"

I stutter, not coming up with a coherent answer. And side note—girlfriends? Really?

"Okay, so who are you hoping doesn't come? Or comes but clearly still doesn't have their stuff together, know what I'm saying?" She covers her smirk when she

D. ALLEN

takes a sip of her drink.

I can't help but laugh with her. Despite how annoying she can be, Daisy was always nice to me. I guess I don't mind her company now and then. In moderation. At the moment, I'm content with our chitchatting. It makes me feel normal. Enough that I let myself indulge in a little gossip.

"Is Christie Harowski still around?"

Daisy's eyes light up. "Oh my God! You didn't hear?"

"No, what happened to her?"

"Okay, so after high school, you know how Christie had gotten accepted to Cornell and was going on and on about how she was going to get her master's degree and blah blah blah? Well, that never happened. She went, but during the first semester she got pregnant by some frat boy. She came back here to have the baby and got a job at Walmart. Okay fine. She was working, providing for the baby. Cool. But then, *apparently*, she got in with this one guy who…let's just say he ran a side business out of his car —"

"Really?" I'm leaning in on the table.

She holds up her hand. "That's what I heard. One way or another, she ended up hooked on God-only-knows what, let the baby cry while she was hyped up on whatever she took. A neighbor heard and called CPS.

The baby went into foster care and she has to have supervised visits."

My mind has officially been blown. She was in the top ten of our class! She had almost a full ride to Cornell! Last time I heard about her, her life was set.

"Damn." I can't hide my smile. It's horrible to get satisfaction off of someone else's misfortune, but she was not a nice person in high school. Karma is real.

"Yup. So even if she does show up, you have nothing to worry about. Actually, you have nothing to worry about with anyone. You're, hands down, *the* most successful person from our class."

I sip my drink, my mood soured a bit. "I don't know if that's true." The conversation has once again slipped back to my lifestyle. Maybe I need to rethink even going to the reunion.

"Tracy, are you kidding me right now? You have—what?—three multiplatinum records, a fourth on the way, and have made millions traveling the world and being this awesome businesswoman. I think you're pretty successful."

"There's more to success than just a career." I turn my attention to the window, watching as the cars navigate the drive-thru in the wet snow that has been smushed to slush.

"Well, you're married, right?"

D. ALLEN

I nod. "Yeah."

She slaps the table and my eyes jerk back to her, nearly spilling my tea all over myself.

"Oh my God! I just got the *best* idea! We should have everyone bring in old pictures for a photo collage! Yeah, we could get everyone's school photos from the yearbooks throughout the years! Ah! It'll be *so cute*!"

I grin. "Not sure how happy some people will be about that, but yeah, it's a great idea." I know I made some horrible fashion choices back in the day. That's why I have a stylist now.

"Maybe some candids, too. That'd be fun. Gosh, there's probably *so many* pictures of you and Steve Austin. You still talk to him?"

Tucking my hair behind my ear, I say, "Uh, not really. I ran into him last night. Quite literally, actually."

"Shut up! Oh, my heart is breaking! Everyone thought you two would get married!"

"Well, I am married. To someone else. Not Steve." I'm not sure if I'm trying to remind Daisy or myself. "And besides, he's probably got a girlfriend or a wife or something too."

Daisy shakes her head. "I don't think so, Trace. Ugh, you two were *so cute*! What happened?"

I finish off my tea. "Um…just grew apart, I guess. Listen, I've gotta run. It was nice seeing you." I pull on

A Christmas Reunion

my coat and give her a wave before heading out the door.

Stephen. If he's single, it makes me wonder what he's been up to for the last ten years. Personally, that is. From what I've seen, he's built a good career for himself. But I can't see him. Not on this trip. Not with everything going on with Charlie. Charlie would get the wrong idea about me wanting a divorce. He'd go to the papers, leak some fictional story.

No. My best option is to stay as far away from Stephen Austin as I possibly can.

Acknowledgments

This project would not have been possible without the support of my Kickstarter backers! Thank you all for your support!

Heiko Koenig
Kathryn Kaleigh
Marlene Renteria
Haley Rhoades
Marguerite
Ashley Webster
Kanyon K.
Franchesca Caram
Gee Rothvoss:)
LJF
Valerie Laing
John Idlor
Jessica Hoyal
Ellis Kaye Creates
Shelbi Courson
Joey Watkins
Jenna
Gary Phillips
Kaitlyn Mehrtens
Giuliana Molinaro
Backer 21

Jessie moved back to picturesque Montana Beach after a heartbreaking split with her ex. She's since thrown herself into her grandparent's inn, which has been struggling financially thanks to the town having seen better days. With few options available, Jessie considers accepting a developer's offer to buy Montana Manor, seeing it as a way to save her family's legacy, until she learns that he wants to tear it down.

Meanwhile, Mason's tired of working at his father's advertising firm in New York City, although his father wants him to become his replacement. Unsure if that's the course he wants his life to take, Mason escapes to Montana Beach and the only inn in town to consider the proposal. But after he meets Jessie, he seems to gain only another reason not to take up his father's offer.

When Mason offers to help Jessie launch a campaign to save Montana Manor, the two quickly find themselves relying more and more on each other. But summer doesn't last forever, and Mason's stay is coming to an end.

Summer Stay is the first book in the Montana Beach series. Available in hardcover, paperback, ebook, and audiobook!

www.DavidNethBooks.com/MontanaBeach

A chance moment. A snow storm. And the gift of a new beginning.

Tristan is ready to party and ring in the New Year by kissing his soon-to-be girlfriend, Julie. The only bad note in his rocking night is the ongoing snow storm. Outside his apartment, he's almost hit by a swerving car! Behind the wheel is Grace, the most beautiful woman with haunting green eyes. She's on her own mission to get home to her grandfather.

In a selfless act reminiscent of the age of knights and chivalry, Tristan vows to get her home…never realizing they are both on a date with destiny and their lives will be forever changed by the SNOW AFTER CHRISTMAS…

www.DavidNethBooks.com/d-allen-standalones

More by the author

To find more books by the author, visit
DavidNethBooks.com/Books

* * *

Subscribe to his newsletter to be the first to know of new
releases and special deals!
DavidNethBooks.com/Newsletter

* * *

If you enjoyed the book, please consider leaving a review
on Goodreads or the retailer you bought it from. Reviews
help potential readers determine whether they'll enjoy a
book, so any comments on what you thought of the story
would be very helpful!

About the Author

D. Allen is the author of the sweet small town romance series, Montana Beach and Small Town Christmas.

Also writes fantasy and superhero fiction as David Neth.

www.DavidNethBooks.com
www.facebook.com/DavidNethBooks
www.instagram.com/dnpublishing

www.ingramcontent.com/pod-product-compliance
Lightning Source LLC
Chambersburg PA
CBHW030656010826
48974CB00008B/855

9 781963 602111